Keith shook his head, gazing at her with wonder. "I've never believed in fate before," he said. "But now, I swear it must be fate that brought you here, into my arms. This was meant to be, Char."

"You're out of your mind."

"Am I? Shall we tempt our fate a little, and see what happens?"

Char's breath caught as Keith lowered his irresistible mouth to her lips. They throbbed with sensation, as if they had hungered only for this moment, and for this man.

Several breathless seconds later, when the kiss came to its honeyed, heart-hammering, spine-tingling conclusion, Char was lost. Keith wasn't exactly calm, cool, or collected, either.

"Wow," he murmured, still cradling her trembling shoulders. "You are the most tempting fate I've ever encountered."

"I thought you said I wasn't your type." Char managed to whisper.

"Did I? I must have been crazy. I guess a man's got to keep an open mind."

She giggled. "Your mind's so open all your marbles have fallen out!"

Keith's low, rich, appreciative laughter echoed in the silence. "You don't pull any punches, do you? Well, I assure you I have not lost my marbles," he said with a tender grin. "Just a small piece of my heart. . . ."

Bantam Books by Kathleen Downes
Ask your bookseller for the titles you have missed.

THE MAN NEXT DOOR
  (Loveswept #49)

PRACTICE MAKES PERFECT
  (Loveswept #93)

WHAT ARE *LOVESWEPT* ROMANCES?

They are stories of true romance and touching emotion. We believe
those two very important ingredients are constants in our highly sensual
and very believable stories in the *LOVESWEPT* line. Our goal is to give
you, the reader, stories of consistently high quality that may sometimes
make you laugh, sometimes make you cry, but are always fresh and
creative and contain many delightful surprises within their pages.

Most romance fans read an enormous number of books. Those they
truly love, they keep. Others may be traded with friends and soon
forgotten. We hope that each *LOVESWEPT* romance will be a
treasure—a "keeper." We will always try to publish

LOVE STORIES YOU'LL NEVER FORGET
BY AUTHORS YOU'LL ALWAYS REMEMBER

The Editors

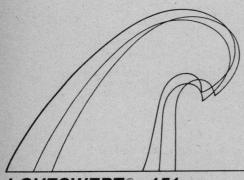

LOVESWEPT® • 151

Kathleen Downes
Char's Webb

BANTAM BOOKS
TORONTO • NEW YORK • LONDON • SYDNEY • AUCKLAND

CHAR'S WEBB

A Bantam Book / August 1986

LOVESWEPT® *and the wave device are registered*
trademarks of Bantam Books, Inc. Registered in U.S. Patent
and Trademark Office and elsewhere.

Cover artwork by Nick Caruso

All rights reserved.
Copyright © 1986 by Kathleen Downes.
Cover artwork copyright © 1986 by Bantam Books, Inc.
This book may not be reproduced in whole or in part, by
mimeograph or any other means, without permission.
For information address: Bantam Books, Inc.

ISBN 0-553-21776-3

Published simultaneously in the United States and Canada

Bantam Books are published by Bantam Books, Inc. Its
trademark, consisting of the words "Bantam Books" and
the portrayal of a rooster, is Registered in U.S. Patent and
Trademark Office and in other countries. Marca Registrada.
Bantam Books, Inc., 666 Fifth Avenue, New York, New
York 10103.

PRINTED IN THE UNITED STATES OF AMERICA

O   0 9 8 7 6 5 4 3 2 1

One

"Hello. I'm Charlotte Smith."

The receptionist went saucer-eyed at Char's announcement. A tense, electric hush fell on the room. The air in the busy office was suddenly humming with a scarcely audible vibration, as if all within earshot had collectively caught their breaths in expectation.

Expectation of what? Char had no idea. Her smile of greeting faltered on her lips. Why was everybody staring at her?

Nervously, she cast a quick, surreptitious glance downward. No, her slip wasn't showing. The buttons of her cream-colored silk blouse hadn't come undone. And her brand-new pair of stockings hadn't run yet.

She was used to getting the occasional second glance from strangers. When you were tall and auburn-haired and reasonably attractive, that happened. People noticed you. But this was something else again. She knew her looks weren't so striking as to bring the activity of an entire office

1

screeching to a halt. Not even here in the quiet little upstate town of Webb Falls, New York.

But *something* had certainly done so. The question was, what? Everything had been proceeding normally until she'd introduced herself.

Oh, dear. The name Charlotte Smith hadn't provoked such a dramatic reaction in years. Not since the day her fifth-grade classmates found out she was named after a talking spider in a storybook.

Somehow, the company grapevine must have found out why she was here. Naturally, everybody was interested in the management consultant brought in from Boston to conduct a three-week study about the feasibility of introducing innovative job-sharing programs and flexitime scheduling at the Webb Company, manufacturer of fine china. Naturally . . . Whom was she trying to kid? Nobody could possibly be *this* interested. What was going on here?

Maybe she could get some answers from the man she was about to meet—the head of the company. Char squared her shoulders beneath the jacket of her blue summer-weight suit. "I'm here to see Mr. Webb," she said firmly. "Mr. Keith W. Webb."

"Oh, my, yes! Yes, of course!" the receptionist said emphatically, looking as pleased and proud as a bird who'd just laid an egg. "I know he'll be thrilled to see *you*." The woman leaned across the desk and added confidingly, "He needs cheering up today, poor man. Is he expecting you, or is this a surprise?"

"I—I'm not quite sure," Char said faintly. "That is, I am a day early, but—"

"So it *is* a surprise." The woman's whole face lit up with delight.

"I guess you could call it that, but . . ." Nervously Char brushed back a tendril of auburn hair that had escaped the neatly coiled knot at the nape of her neck. *What was going on here*? Did the pleasant, motherly-looking woman at the receptionist's desk greet *everyone* like this? That is, as if they were unexpected packages wrapped up in fancy paper and tied with ribbons, ready to be presented to the boss? And how could Mr. Webb possibly be cheered, much less "thrilled," by the arrival of Charlotte Smith?

He didn't sound thrilled.

"I thought I told you I didn't want to be disturbed until after the two o'clock meeting." The man's bearlike growl was so loud, Char couldn't help overhearing. And because the office was equipped with an outdated intercom system, she could hear everything else he said too.

"But, Mr. Webb, there's somebody special here to see you—somebody I know you'll want to see!" the receptionist chirped coyly into the intercom. She slipped Char a knowing grin, but Char was gnawing too hard at her lower lip to grin back.

"I wouldn't bet on it," the intimidating voice rasped out. "But whoever it is, he'll have to wait until after the damn meeting."

The receptionist gave Char a broad, reassuring wink. "Of course, Mr. Webb," she said, with just a trace of mischief in her voice. "I'll tell *Ms. Charlotte . . . Smith* that she'll have to come back another time."

"*What?*" The harsh explosion of sound from the intercom took Char by surprise. Once again it seemed that her name had triggered a most unexpected reaction. "*Who?*"

"Charlotte Smith." The woman grinned triumphantly. "Shall I send her in?"

There were four seconds of total silence. "By all means. Send her in."

Something about the quiet enunciation of the words sent a chill up Char's spine. When the receptionist gave her a warm, conspiratorial smile and gestured to the door beyond the desk, she had to fight the urge to take to her heels and run.

What would she be walking into when she walked through that door? She threw a hasty glance over her shoulder and saw that every pair of eyes in the room was watching her.

She lifted her chin defiantly and marched forward. She'd been hired to do a job here, and she intended to do it. No petty tyrant was going to get away with bullying her! But—oh, dear—how she wished she knew what was going on!

She turned the doorknob and stepped into the room.

Instantly a rough male hand yanked the door out of her grasp and slammed it shut behind her.

"Who the hell are you and who put you up to this?"

Char sucked in a breath of air and simply stared, dumbfounded, at the large male creature glaring down at her so furiously. He was the most stunningly handsome man she had ever seen in her whole life.

"I said, who *are* you?" His quiet, gravelly voice awoke a tremor in her very bones. His blazing eyes of pale jade green were brilliant and hard as polished stone.

She gulped. A fluttery sensation invaded her as she looked up into the man's face—a lean, strong face with a firm jaw, cleft chin, and high cheekbones. Glossy black hair tumbled over his forehead in unruly locks, adding a touch of rebellion to the conventional image presented by his crisp white shirt, dark suit, and tie.

Get a grip, Char, she mentally cautioned herself. He was still waiting for her to answer his curt question.

"I'm Charlotte Smith, and I'm—"

"The hell you are!"

His contemptuous response suddenly triggered Char's sense of humor. She planted her hands on her hips and grinned. "Are you saying I'm *not* Charlotte Smith?"

"Precisely."

She laughed, a trifle breathlessly. "That's crazy. *You're* crazy! I've been Charlotte Smith for twenty-nine years. And I've got a driver's license, a passport, and a birth certificate to prove it!"

He gave an impatient shrug, dismissing everything she'd said. "Just what is it you're hoping to gain by this charade?"

Char began to feel annoyed. Not to mention very confused. "What gives you the right to accuse me of lying about my own name? How would *you* know who I am, anyway? You and I are total strangers to each other."

"Precisely my point."

"It *is*?" She gave him a doubtful glance. Funny, she thought, he didn't *look* deranged.

"I've never seen you before in my life." He obviously thought *that* clinched his whole argument. Char was utterly baffled.

"So?" she prompted. It didn't seem like an unreasonable question to her. But instantly the man's face went grim and pale with fury.

"Exactly what are you implying?"

Oh, dear. When he talked through clenched teeth like that, he sounded so . . . menacing. Char began to have serious doubts about his sanity.

"I didn't mean to imply anything!" she hastily informed him. "Mr. Webb," she pleaded, trying to stay calm, "don't you think we could sit down and talk this over like two rational, mature adults?"

"By all means." His words had an ironic edge to them, and Char continued to feel very uneasy as she sat in the chair he indicated. "Now," he said, standing over her with his arms folded across his broad chest. "I want you to explain what's going on."

"But I haven't the faintest idea! *You're* the one who ought to be explaining things! And I do wish you'd sit down." It made her feel quite dizzy to look up the whole gorgeous length of him to that hard, sensual mouth and those intense green eyes.

He scarcely seemed to have heard her. "Why are you claiming to be someone we both know you can't possibly be?"

"But I—"

"Please! No more lies. There's no point." He gave a wry, enigmatic smile. "After all, I *am* rather intimately acquainted with the *true* Charlotte Smith."

For a stunned second, Char found herself doubting *her* sanity. Nothing made sense anymore. But suddenly a glimmer of light began to dawn.

"There must be two of us!"

"What?"

"Two Charlotte Smiths. Don't you see? It's the only explanation!"

"Impossible."

"But why? Smith isn't exactly an unusual last name. And there are a fair number of Charlottes in the world, too."

"I'm not a great believer in coincidences, Ms. Whoever-you-are. And you'll never convince me that you just *happened* to waltz in here calling yourself Charlotte Smith!"

"Of course it didn't just happen. Your company hired me, remember? Unless . . ." A sickening thought occurred to her. "Oh, no! If I got this contract because you thought I was that *other* Charlotte Smith—the one you're so 'intimately' acquainted with—then you ought to be ashamed of the way you do business, Mr. Webb! That kind of unprofessional—"

"Hold it! What are you talking about? When did we hire you? *What* contract?" A look of horror was dawning in the keen, jade-colored eyes.

"The contract for the feasibility study of job-sharing and flexitime scheduling, Mr. Webb. Brannon-Hale, the consulting firm I work for, submitted a job proposal on this project four months ago, and you awarded us the contract."

"Four months ago?" His voice seemed to falter. Char nodded, and he swallowed. Beads of perspiration were suddenly visible on his forehead. "Did that job proposal happen to mention your name, Ms. Smith?"

He'd called her Ms. Smith! Did that mean he was finally starting to believe her? If so, he wasn't looking too happy about it.

"Of course. My résumé was included as part of the proposal."

"I see." He covered his forehead with his open palm and let his hand slide slowly down his face. Then he gave a short, harsh bark of laughter. "Oh, boy," was all he said.

Char watched, puzzled, as he stepped to his desk and began rummaging through stacks of file folders and loose papers. At last he seemed to find what he was looking for, and he flipped the file open and studied it in silence for several minutes.

He looked up once or twice for a quick, assessing glance at her, and she realized he was reading her résumé. She felt faintly uncomfortable at this, though she knew he would find nothing of a personal or revealing nature about her there. And he would certainly see that her qualifications for this assignment were excellent.

He closed the folder, and sighed. "You're not even my type," he said.

"I beg your pardon!" she exclaimed in icy indignation. Of course she wasn't his type—a man as good-looking as he was probably consorted only with ravishingly beautiful women. But what did that have to do with the job she'd been hired for?

"You've got possibilities, though," he added thoughtfully. "And the timing couldn't be better."

"Thanks." Her tone was one of withering sarcasm. "Let's get one thing straight, Mr. Webb—"

"Are you married?"

"Now, listen here—"

"Are you?"

"No. But what—"

"Engaged?"

"No. What is this? An interrogation?"

"Living with anyone?"

"No! And you have no legal or ethical right to ask me these questions!"

"True." Surprisingly, he grinned, and Char felt a quick, disturbing flutter inside when she saw what that grin did to his already handsome face. He was breathtaking. Literally breathtaking. *Too bad he's a client*, she found herself thinking. She'd made it her policy never to get involved with clients, and she'd avoided a lot of trouble that way.

"What about you?" **she** asked impulsively. "Are *you* married or engaged?" So much for avoiding trouble.

His grin widened. "Why do you ask?"

Her cheeks turned pink. She *shouldn't* have asked, she knew. Someone ought to be maintaining this conversation on a dignified, professional level. Oh, well. It was too late for that now.

"Just answer, yes or no," she ordered tartly. But she was sure she knew his answer already. With her rotten luck, he *had* to be married. Or at least engaged. It never failed. Whenever she met a man who set her pulses stirring, he always turned out to be firmly attached to some other woman. And *this* man definitely stirred her pulses. Even if he was a client.

"Why don't we discuss it over coffee?" he suggested with a seductive smile.

Oh, dear. Any man whose marital status was so complicated that it had to be explained over coffee was someone to avoid. Especially when he had such fascinating green eyes and such a potent smile. And especially when he was a client, she reminded herself. "Mr. Webb—"

"Call me Keith." His hand was on her arm, gently but firmly assisting her to her feet.

"Mr. Webb," she persisted. "We have nothing to discuss but the project I was hired to complete."

"We can talk about that too," he said agreeably. "But don't you want me to unravel for you the mystery of the 'other' Charlotte Smith? Aren't you even curious?"

Char hesitated beneath his gaze. She did want to hear about the other Charlotte. And she noticed there were no rings on Keith Webb's large, tanned, shapely hands. Of course, that didn't *prove* he wasn't married. And he was still her client. But she was only agreeing to a cup of coffee, after all. Nothing more.

"Very well," she said.

"Very well, *Keith*," he corrected. Stepping to his desk, he switched on the intercom. "Cancel the two o'clock meeting, Beth. Ms. Smith and I are taking the rest of the afternoon off."

"Right, Mr. Webb," the receptionist replied happily.

"Wait a minute!" said Char. "You can't cancel a meeting just to have coffee with—"

"But I already have." He smiled.

"Wasn't the meeting pretty important, though?" she asked worriedly. "I mean, you sounded so grouchy about being interrupted—" She broke off, flushing with embarrassment. Oh, dear. She'd just accused her new client of grouchiness. Of course, it was true, but that didn't make it a tactful thing to say.

"Believe me, it wasn't the meeting I was grouchy about. Come on, let's go."

Full of misgivings and unquenchable curiosity, Char let herself be whisked out the rear door of his office and into an elevator. After a swift downward journey, the elevator doors parted to reveal the starkly lit gloom of the underground parking garage, and Char drew back in dismay.

"When you said 'coffee,' I assumed you meant somewhere at the plant."

"That's because you've never tasted what passes for coffee here at the plant. It's on my list of things to change now that I'm in charge, but a new phone system has to come first. That, and possibly a new work schedule, which is what we've hired you to evaluate."

"I see. You must have become head of the company fairly recently, then."

"Six months ago. My father took early retirement, and now he and Mom are fulfilling their life-long dream of sailing around the world together."

"How nice for them. Nice for you too," she added, somewhat cynically.

"Not really. Coming back to Webb Falls to take on the family business was a responsibility I hadn't counted on for another few years. To tell the truth, I was perfectly happy in Chicago, running my own business. But family is family, so here I am."

Char hoped he didn't expect her to feel *sorry* for him. The man had been made head of a very prosperous company without having to lift a finger, just because he was the boss's son. And now he had the gall to talk as if he were doing *them* a favor, instead of the other way round! She had to admit, though, that he didn't seem like the type who'd want things handed to him on a silver platter. He was too dynamic for that.

He led her toward a row of cars presided over by a uniformed attendant. Obviously this was a private parking area for the Webb Company management; each parking space was labeled with the name and title of a company official, and the cars themselves were large, well-polished luxury models. Except for one.

Keith Webb opened the passenger door of the mud-splashed red pickup truck and cleared a pair of mud-caked work boots off the floor, tossing them into the back. He grinned at Char as he took her arm once more, and his fingers felt warm and strong through the light fabric of her suit jacket as he helped her into the pickup. But that was no excuse, she reminded herself sternly, for the warm, tingling awareness that traveled up and down her spine at his touch.

"The head of the company drives a pickup?" She lifted her brows quizzically.

"Among other things." He unknotted his dark silk tie and stuffed it carelessly in his pocket, then turned the key in the ignition. "Sorry about the mud. I was out early this morning mending some fences, and the ground was still soft from last night's rain."

Char blinked. "Mending fences?"

"On my farm."

"Farm?" It occurred to Char that she was beginning to sound like a rather unintelligent parrot. But she couldn't believe what she was hearing. What could this urbane man in the elegantly tailored dark suit have to do with farming and fence-mending? He certainly hadn't picked up *those* skills in Chicago.

"I see by your expression that you agree with

Uncle Eliot and Aunt Agnes," he said dryly. "You think the head of the Webb Company has no business living on a farm, getting his hands dirty tending livestock and mending fences. He should uphold the family dignity by settling down in a mansion on Maple Street and marrying the mayor's daughter."

"Huh? My expression couldn't possibly have told you that!" Especially not the part about the mayor's daughter, she thought, watching his competent hands on the steering wheel as he drove up the ramp of the parking garage, out into the afternoon sunshine. "I've never even met your aunt and uncle. And why should I care where you live or whom you marry?" she demanded crossly, knowing in her heart of hearts that she *did* care, just a little. Even though he was a client.

"You're right," he admitted sheepishly. "Please forgive me—I've gotten a little touchy on that particular subject lately."

"More like a *lot* touchy, I'd say."

"Okay, a *lot* touchy," he conceded. "And you would be, too, if you were the object of a friendly conspiracy to marry you off to someone you had no desire to marry!" His voice was raw with tension and frustration, and his green eyes flashed.

"My goodness," said Char. "That does sound . . . upsetting." Then she looked at him thoughtfully, crinkling her nose in puzzlement. "But I'm surprised you haven't put a stop to it. I've only just met you, but frankly, you seem like a very forceful man. I can't see you letting other people push you where you don't want to go." She wasn't quite sure *how* she knew it, but she knew it.

"You're very observant," he said, and Char felt his eyes on her, observing *her* with a deeper interest than before. "Unfortunately," he continued, turning his attention back to the road, "there are complications. You see, I care for these people. I don't want to hurt them. And in my efforts to get myself out of this mess in the kindest way possible, I seem to have made matters worse. Much worse," he added gloomily. "If you only knew half of—"

He broke off abruptly and threw Char a quick, unreadable glance. If she'd seen that look, she might have demanded a detailed explanation right then and there. But she was too busy trying to put things together in her own mind.

"Does this little matchmaking conspiracy you're so touchy about have anything to do with the reception I got when I showed up at your office?" she asked.

Keith's high cheekbones flared with color. "I'm afraid it has *everything* to do with it," he confessed. "And before we go any further, I want to say that I'm truly sorry for the way I acted, Charlotte." He said her name tentatively, exploringly, and his eyes met hers with a look of genuine chagrin and apology. "My behavior was . . ."

He seemed at a loss for words, but Char certainly was not.

"Your behavior was rude and outrageous!" she informed him. "I was quite convinced I was dealing with a raving lunatic. And you may call me Char." She glanced hastily away, feeling suddenly shy with him. "All my friends do."

"Thank you. I'd very much like to be your friend, Char." He gave her a wry yet intimate smile. "But I'm not sure you'll want to be *my* friend once you hear what that little scene in my office was all about."

"Try me," she said. She had a funny feeling that no matter what Keith said next, she'd still want him . . . um—want him for a *friend*, that is. Even though he was a client.

"I thought you were part of the plot," he said.

"*Me?* Part of the plot to get you to marry the mayor's daughter?" Char exclaimed. Keith nodded. "Why on earth would you think that?"

He grimaced uncomfortably. "Here comes the tricky part for me to explain: my involvement with Charlotte Smith. The 'other' Charlotte Smith, if you will."

"Oh," Char said in a hollow voice. Oh, dear, she thought. The other Charlotte Smith—the one he was so intimate with—had completely slipped her mind once she'd climbed into Keith's pickup truck. That was a bad sign. And now she felt thoroughly depressed at the prospect of hearing about his involvement with this other woman. That was a very bad sign indeed. The man's love life should be no concern of hers. After all, he was a client.

"Well, maybe it's none of my business," she said.

"I'm afraid it *is* your business," he said gloomily. "You see, I . . . uh . . . oh, hell! There's no easy way to explain this."

"Then you'd better wait till I've fortified myself with that cup of coffee you promised me. I get the feeling I'm going to need it."

"You could be right. Anyway, we're almost there."

Char glanced out the window and saw to her surprise that they'd left the shady, tree-lined streets of the town behind. They were driving through a scenic countryside of gently rolling, wooded hills and lush green fields and pastures.

"Pardon my curiosity, but isn't this an awfully long way to drive for a cup of coffee?"

"*My* coffee is worth driving a few extra miles for," he said complacently. "I'm the only guy in town who uses freshly ground coffee beans. Everybody else gets their coffee out of a jar or can."

"You mean you're taking me to your house?" Char asked in dismay.

"Yep. Here we are." They drove up a shaded gravel drive to an old, two-story white frame farmhouse. Lilac bushes edged the broad front porch, and a broad swathe of clover-dotted lawn circled the house.

Char felt as if she'd just stepped into a Norman Rockwell print. The air smelled fresh and sweet with the scent of growing things, still moist from last night's rain. It was hard to believe that only two weeks ago she'd been finishing an assignment in L.A., battling freeway traffic and breathing smog-choked air.

"What do you think of it?" Keith asked eagerly.

"It's beautiful." She spoke the simple truth. The house was on a gradual rise of land, with views of orchards, corn fields, and pastures in all directions. Just down the slope beyond the house, a large red barn completed the picture of rural tranquility. "It must be quite a change from your life in Chicago."

"It is. And I love it."

"I can see why," she said softly. Turning back to the man beside her, she found his penetrating green eyes regarding her with an expression she couldn't quite decipher. A slow smile crinkled the corners of his mouth and eyes.

"I'm glad you like it," he said. "I wasn't sure you would. After all, according to your résumé, you've spent the last five years in one city after another."

"Unfortunately, I have," Char agreed with a sigh. "The consulting firm I work for is based in Boston, but they send us on assignments all over the map. Usually to big cities. Six weeks in Denver, a month in Chicago, a week in Atlanta, three months in L.A. I'm always living out of a suitcase." And she hadn't realized until this very minute that she was starting to grow weary of living that way. When had it stopped being a challenge, an adventure, and started turning into drudgery?

"It sounds rather grim," Keith said. "And lonely. But then again . . ." His mouth twisted in a pensive smile. "A person can be lonely anywhere. Even in the town where he grew up, surrounded by people who've known him all his life."

Was he talking about himself? And if so, was he *serious*? Char refused to believe that any man so heart-throbbingly handsome had to bother his gorgeous head about loneliness, of all things!

Loneliness was for more ordinary mortals, such as Char herself. And she had to admit, there'd been some lonely times lately. What chance was there for any sort of serious, committed, potentially permanent relationship, when she never stayed in one place long enough even to memorize the area code?

At least she wasn't desperate enough to settle for something temporary, just to keep the bed warm at night. Her electric blanket did that job just fine, thank you very much! But that didn't mean she hadn't been tempted . . .

"You've gotten awfully quiet all of a sudden," Keith said. "Have *you* been lonely, Char?" The way he said her name, it was almost like a caress. His eyes were softer now, understanding. She felt an odd jolt of panic. Those eyes of his had the power to strip naked her most private thoughts and feelings.

"I love my work," she said. "And everywhere I go, I meet warm, friendly, interesting people. We have a lot of fun together." Everything she said was true. But . . .

"You haven't answered my question," Keith said gently.

Char bristled. "I've worked very hard to build a successful career. I don't have *time* to be lonely."

Keith did not look convinced, but he merely

shrugged his shoulders and changed the subject. "Before we go inside for coffee, would you like a quick tour of the farm?"

"I'd love it," she said, relieved that his attention would no longer be focused on her. "And I'm curious to hear how you find time to run a farm like this in addition to heading such a successful company."

"There's a simple answer to that. I don't try to run the farm—I've got a damn good manager who does it for me. But I try to do my share of the work around the place, because I get so much satisfaction out of it."

"Keeping in touch with nature and all that?" she asked, panting a little in her efforts to keep up with his long-legged stride as he headed down the gravel drive toward the barn. Her high heeled shoes were definitely not designed for walking in mud and gravel.

"You may think it's corny, Char. But yes, that's how I feel. When you work with the land, you see the miracle of birth, death, and regeneration happening all around you, every day. It puts things in perspective."

"I don't think that's corny at all," she said, hurrying to catch up with him.

"You don't?" He stopped abruptly, and eagerly turned to face her, just as she put on a heroic burst of speed.

"Oh!" she said as her body collided with his. The soft weight of her breasts jostled against his broad, hard chest, and she instinctively gripped his waist to keep from falling. At the same instant, he caught her shoulders in a supportive hold. Oh, dear. Hot tingles and warm blushes flared up and down her flesh.

Keith's jade-green eyes were distinctly amused as they looked down into her flushed face. But there was a trace of something more—an answering flare of sexual awareness. Char yanked her hands away from the hard, muscled curve of his waist as if she'd just touched a hot stove.

"Sorry," she mumbled.

"Don't be sorry." With a light but lingering caress of his hands on her shoulders, he released her. "It was my fault. I shouldn't have stopped so suddenly." But his polite words of apology were belied by the message in his eyes. *Don't be sorry we touched each other*, his eyes said. *Because I'm glad we did, and I'm going to do it again soon . . . on purpose.*

Char felt a wave of dizziness wash over her. It was happening too fast, this mushrooming attraction between them. This man was her client. She hardly knew him. She didn't even know yet if she trusted him.

And how *could* she trust a man with such brilliant green eyes, and such long, velvety lashes, and such a sexy, sexy smile? She took another long, appreciative look, just to reconfirm all those untrustworthy traits. Mmm, yes. Deep, glowing green eyes the color of a storm-tossed sea. A woman could drown in those eyes. . . .

"Char?"

"Mmm?"

"Is there a fly on my nose, or something? You've been staring at my face for at least half a minute."

"Oh!" Char gulped with embarrassment. "I must have been daydreaming about something else." She didn't really expect him to believe her. With a face and body like his, he probably caught women ogling him all the time.

"Is that one of your chickens?" she asked hastily, pointing to a plump fowl strutting in the barnyard. *Anything* to divert Keith's attention from the fact that she'd been drooling over him like a love-sick teenager.

Her ruse seemed to work. Keith was more than ready to show her his chickens, geese, pigs, and dairy cows, and his enthusiasm was contagious. As they toured the barn, from hayloft to milking room to pigpen, Char found herself hanging on his every word.

She tried to convince herself that this was only because what he had to say was so fascinating. Her interest had nothing to do with the way his green eyes sparkled and his face lit up with animation as he talked. It had nothing to do with the deep, resonant timbre of his voice, which made listening to him so pleasurable. No indeed.

But try as she might, she couldn't deny the troubling sexual spark that had ignited between them. She felt its presence in the dim, dusty, hay-scented air of the barn. It caused her nerves to quiver sweetly like the plucked strings of a harp each time he stood close to her or touched her arm. It made her nervous. Nervous and clumsy. And that, combined with her high heels and the treacherous walking conditions, resulted in catastrophe.

Two

They had just emerged from the cool, dusky half-light inside the barn, out into the dazzling afternoon sunshine. Half-blinded by the brightness, Char panicked when Keith moved up close behind her. Trying to sidestep away from him like a skittish mare, she tripped and went sprawling forward on her hands and knees in a patch of mud.

"Oh, dear," she muttered, staring down at the muddy ground only a few inches from her nose. There went another brand-new pair of stockings! And the cleaning bill for her suit would be horrendous.

"Char! Are you all right?" Two strong hands circled her waist and urgently hauled her to her feet again. Anxiously, Keith inspected her hands and knees for cuts and scrapes.

"There's nothing wrong with me that a little soap and water won't cure," she declared self-consciously, trying to tug her muddy hands out of his grasp. This was *so* embarrassing.

"Then I'd better get you to some soap and water, right away!" Before she could even guess what he had in mind, Keith swept her up in his arms and settled her snugly against his chest.

"Keith, *no*! This is ridiculous! I'm getting mud all over your suit!"

"I never did like this suit much." He was carrying her up the driveway, toward the house. The grip of his powerful arms and the easy rhythm of his stride made her feel like some frail, delicate, weightless creature. Which was far from the truth, as she well knew, but it was a deliciously pleasant illusion nonetheless.

His body's potent warmth and muscled firmness pressed close against her cheek. His subtle, masculine scent teased her nostrils. When he bent his head to look down into her upturned face, Char felt breathless beneath the lambent green fire of his gaze.

The pace of his footsteps slowed, and then stopped altogether. A disturbing tremor that could have been either fear or desire swept through Char like a seismic wave. She knew she had to get her feet back on solid ground without delay.

"Put me down this minute!" she demanded shakily.

Keith shook his head, gazing at her with the bemused wonder of a child who has just captured a glimmering firefly.

"Can't you feel it, Char?"

Her tongue froze in panic, but she gave a desperate shake of her head. Whatever he was feeling, she wanted no part of it.

"I've never believed in fate before," he said. "But now I swear it must be fate that brought you here, into my arms. This was meant to be, Char."

"You're out of your mind."

"Am I? Shall we tempt our fate a little, and see what happens?"

Char's breath caught in her throat as Keith lowered his sensuous, irresistible mouth to her plain, ordinary lips. Only, they didn't feel plain or ordinary at all, once the kiss began. They throbbed with sensation, as if they had hungered and thirsted only for this moment, and for this man.

Her feet slid to the ground as Keith freed his hands for a long, slow, stroking caress of her back and shoulders. His kiss deepened into an intimate, intoxicating exchange of nectared pleasure. Char felt an enervating warmth and wooziness spreading inside her, as if she'd just belted down a shot of straight tequila.

Her worst fears were confirmed. Keith Webb was every bit as good to touch as he was to look at. And Char was every bit as susceptible as she'd feared. But, oh, Lord, she was loving every minute of it!

Several long, breathless seconds later, the kiss came to its honeyed, heart-hammering, spine-tingling conclusion. By then, Char wasn't thinking too clearly anymore. And from the looks of him, Keith wasn't exactly calm, cool, or collected, either.

"Wow," he said weakly, still cradling her trembling shoulders with his hands. "You are the most tempting fate I've ever encountered!"

"I thought you said I wasn't your type." Her tone was amazingly spunky for a woman whose legs were momentarily too wobbly to support her own weight.

"Did I? I must have been crazy. It just goes to show, a man's got to keep an open mind."

She giggled. "Your mind's so open, all your marbles have fallen out!"

The words were spoken before Char could stop herself, and she was aghast. She scarcely knew this man. He was her new *client*, for crying out loud! And now she'd just insulted him in the same irreverent, shoot-from-the-hip, bantering style she usually reserved for her nearest and dearest friends.

Oh, dear. He was sure to take offense. Maybe if she explained that she was still in a state of shock from being kissed completely senseless . . .

Keith's low, rich, appreciative laughter interrupted her worried thoughts. "You don't believe in pulling your punches, do you? Well, I can assure you, I have *not* lost my marbles." He gave her a crinkly grin. "Just a small piece of my heart, Char."

Ohh, he was good. That line probably reduced most women to putty in his hands. But not Char. She was made of sterner stuff. Her heart merely did a quiet flip-flop, and her breathing couldn't have stopped for more than twenty seconds, max.

Keith spoke again before Char had quite recovered her powers of speech. "Let's get you to the house, where you can clean up," he suggested matter-of-factly.

His arms were already slipping around her to lift her again, when Char came to her senses.

"I'll walk!" she said hastily, backing away.

He gave a cheerful shrug. "As you wish." They started up the driveway toward the house.

Twenty minutes later, Char turned off the antique brass taps of the claw-footed bathtub, and reached out through the shower curtains surrounding the tub to clutch at a fluffy blue bath towel.

It felt marvelous to be clean again. But now what was she going to wear? Her suit was hopelessly wet and muddy. Keith had promised to lend her some clothes, but where were they? Did he expect her to prance around the house half-naked in order to find them?

Char sighed. Who *knew* what that insane man expected, with all his crazy talk about fate bringing them together? She pressed a finger to her still-throbbing lips, and smiled in spite of herself. His kisses were dangerous. If she was going to run the risk of sharing any more of them, she'd better be wearing more than just a towel!

Draping the towel carefully around her body, she stepped to the bathroom door and peered into the hallway.

"Keith?" she called softly.

No response.

"I'm ready for those clothes now, Mr. Webb."

Utter silence. The afternoon sunlight streamed across the rich golden oak of the floorboards in the hall. The aroma of freshly ground French-roast coffee wafted up the stairs. But there was no sound of any human presence.

She raised her voice. "Yoo-hoo. Mr. Webb?"

The sound echoed faintly back from all the nooks and crannies of the huge old farmhouse.

This was getting ridiculous! She was fuming. She refused to remain cowering in the bathroom like a Victorian maiden. If Keith Webb was too unspeakably rude to provide her with a change of clothes, she'd just have to find some for herself.

Gripping the towel, she tiptoed down the hall and into the first room she came to. Keith's bedroom. Even without the slightly muddied dark business suit tossed in a heap on the floor, she would have known. The warmth and vitality of the man seemed to linger in the spacious, sunlit room.

She took a deep breath and headed for the closet. Her footsteps sounded unnaturally loud in the empty, silent house. She felt like a trespasser, snooping around in Keith's room. But she had to have something to wear, didn't she? Still, her hand was trembling guiltily as she reached for the handle of the closet door.

Brrr-ring!

Char gave a small shriek and whirled to face the doorway. Only when she saw no one there did she realize the noise came from the telephone by the bed.

She stood frozen while the phone continued to ring. As she counted the sixth ring, it became clear that Keith wasn't going to answer it. He didn't even seem to be in the house. She walked over to the bed and picked up the receiver.

"Hello?"

There was a faint, choked gasp on the other end of the line, and then silence.

Oh, dear. Whom had she just mortally offended by answering Keith's phone? His Aunt Agnes? The mayor's daughter? The other Charlotte Smith?

"Hello?" she repeated hesitantly, wondering if she should start explaining who she was and the perfectly innocent reason for her to be standing here next to Keith's bed, wearing nothing but a blue towel, taking Keith's phone calls. On second thought, perhaps she'd better *not* explain. She settled for saying, "Keith Webb's residence—may I help you?"

"So it's true." The young woman's tearful voice was bleak with despair.

Oh, dear. Char's heart knotted with pity and dismay. "Oh, please! Don't jump to any conclusions! I'm sure—"

"You're Charlotte Smith, aren't you?" The caller made it sound like an accusation.

"Well, yes. But—"

"Then I'm not jumping to conclusions! It's you that Keith loves, and—"

"He does?" The question popped out before Char

could restrain herself, but fortunately the caller paid no attention.

"—and now you're l-living with him!" The caller sobbed.

"I am *not* living with him! I only just m—"

"And you're engaged to be m-married to him, aren't you?"

"Of course n—" Once again her indignant denial was cut off.

"He told me about you four months ago, but I refused to believe him. I thought he was just making it up. But I was only kidding myself. I should have known Keith could never love a cripple like me. Nobody could." The voice broke into noisy sobs.

Char was speechless with pity and anger and confusion. She wanted to say something comforting to this poor, pathetic girl whose heart Keith Webb had so obviously broken. But what could she say? Though she could truthfully insist that *she* wasn't engaged to or living with or otherwise involved with Keith Webb, what about the *other* Charlotte Smith? It seemed clear that Keith was very involved with *her*. And that made Char furious. He'd had no right to kiss her the way he had this afternoon, if he was in love with someone else. And all that talk about fate! The man was a snake.

"He's not worth your tears," she said at last, after long, painful minutes of listening to the girl's steady sobbing.

"Easy for you to say," the caller said with a sniff. "You're the one who's got him! And you obviously don't care that your happiness is at my expense." There was a loud click as she hung up.

Slowly Char put the receiver down. She felt sorry for that girl, whoever she was, but there was no denying the kid had a lot of growing up to do. No woman with an ounce of self-respect would have made that phone call. But no doubt Keith was to blame for that—playing fast and loose with a vulnerable young girl's affections, until she didn't have any pride left. The more Char thought about it, the angrier she got.

And to think that if it hadn't been for that phone call, she herself might have been taken in by that silver-tongued swamp rat, that green-eyed louse, that—

"That towel never looked better," Keith's deep voice drawled from the bedroom doorway. "It matches your eyes."

But it wasn't her *eyes* he was looking at, she noticed. In spite of her anger, she couldn't help catching her breath as she was struck all over again by how marvelous he looked, wearing jeans and a faded blue cotton shirt. No man should be that handsome.

"I loathe and despise you," she said in icy, measured tones.

"Say what?" For a second he looked as stunned as if a brick wall had just fallen on top of him. Then he shrugged. "Well, that's a start." His grin was mischievous. "At least you're not indifferent to me."

"Ohh! You are a rat, a sneak, and a creep, and if I never see you again, it'll be too soon!"

Keith clutched at his chest and swayed backward in the doorway, dropping the bundle of clothes he'd been carrying. "Say it's not so." He groaned with a melodramatic flourish.

"I'm glad you think it's so funny. That's just the attitude I would have expected from a—" *Oh, dear.* She stopped short as the realization hit her—Keith Webb's personal life was technically none of her business.

Much as she might itch to tell him just what she thought of his behavior, she had to consider their professional, working relationship. She'd been hired as a management consultant, period. In other words, if her client chose to act like pond scum in his personal affairs, it wasn't her job to tell him so. She was supposed to stay polite and professional even if it killed her.

Keith seemed more amused than offended as he studied her furious red face. "Don't stop now, Char! Spit it out—say what's on your mind. I can take it . . . I think. What were you going to call me just now?"

"A heartless philanderer," she muttered.

"A *what*?"

"You heard me."

"I heard you, but I can't believe you're serious! Are you mad because I kissed you, Char? That kiss was a very *sincere*, unphilandering kiss, I assure you. And not at all heartless."

She might have fallen for his coaxing, charming smile if she hadn't known it was false as a hooker's glued-on eyelashes. "You disgust me," she said. So much for trying to be polite and professional!

He stared at her with a very puzzled look on his face. "Correct me if I'm wrong, but weren't we getting along just fine a mere thirty minutes ago? What the hell happened?"

"While you were out, a young woman called."

"And that makes me a philanderer?" he asked incredulously.

"Don't play games with me. That girl was tied up in knots over you."

He winced. "You must mean Debbie. Just because I'm the unwilling object of a nineteen-year-old's unrequited passion doesn't mean I'm a heartless rat, Char. I'm sorry she's hurting, but what can I do? Whatever she told you—"

"She didn't tell me much of anything. But when she found out my name, she seemed to think I was living with you and that we were practically engaged!"

"Oh, hell, I should have guessed. No wonder you're upset." He looked embarrassed and apologetic. "Damn. I wanted to explain it to you myself."

Char was speechless. But only for as long as it took to catch her breath. "Listen, buster! All the explaining in the world isn't going to make it okay that you kissed me the way you did!"

"You seemed to think it was more than just 'okay' at the time," he reproachfully reminded her. "I know *I* did. That kiss was something special, far beyond a mere 'okay.' "

"Ohhh! I *knew* I couldn't trust a man with such long eyelashes. Have you no shame? At the time you kissed me, I had no idea you were practically *engaged* to the other Charlotte Smith!"

Keith let out an explosive hoot of laughter. "Don't tell me you actually think—" He took one look at her face, and sobered instantly. "Obviously, you *do* think it," he concluded aloud, staring thoughtfully at her. Then he took a step forward. "Char, there's something—"

"Don't come any closer, you . . . you reprobate!" She clutched the towel around her body, wishing passionately that her shoulders and thighs weren't bare to his gaze. Even the parts of her that were covered felt vulnerable. After all, a towel could so easily be stripped away. Just like her self-respect, if she let this man touch her again.

"Char, I'm not engaged to anyone. Or living with anyone. Or even romantically involved with any other woman at this point in my life. And there is no—"

"I don't believe you," Char cut in belligerently. "Why would that girl—Debbie—say you were involved with Charlotte Smith if you're not?"

To her astonishment, the man's ears turned red.

He stared longingly at the floor as if wishing a trapdoor would miraculously open under his feet and swallow him up. Ah-ha, Char thought. He was obviously guilty as charged. So why did she feel so disappointed?

But then he cleared his throat and spoke in a slightly muffled voice. "Would you believe it's because I told her one small, well-intentioned lie that's backfired like a stick of dynamite?"

"What are you talking about? What lie?"

He rubbed the back of his neck. "It's a complicated story. How about if you come downstairs and have some of that coffee—"

"Nothing doing. Tell me now."

"Right." She saw his Adam's apple move as he swallowed. "It all started when I moved back to Webb Falls six months ago. Or maybe it started when I was twelve years old and Debbie was still a red, wrinkled, squalling infant wrapped in a pink blanket. My Aunt Agnes and Debbie's mother, the mayor's wife, put their heads together and decided it would be just the cutest thing if Debbie and I got married someday."

"Wait a minute. You mean, *Debbie* is the mayor's daughter? *She's* the one everybody expects you to—"

"Of course she is. I thought you had that figured out for yourself," he said impatiently.

"Um, not exactly. But go on."

"Well, I had no idea what they were planning. To me, Debbie Forrest was like a much-younger kid sister. When I left town to go to college, she was starting kindergarten. When I was starting my own business, she was graduating from sixth grade. Sixth grade, for crying out loud!" He shook his head in disbelief. "How could anyone in his or her right mind possibly think . . ."

"But when you came back six months ago, she was all grown up, wasn't she?" Char suggested.

"That depends on your definition of grown up. To me, she was still the toddler who'd tried to eat my math homework!" He sighed. "But when I arrived in Webb Falls to take over from my father, Debbie was going through a very rough time. My aunt and uncle asked if I'd mind spending some time with her, trying to cheer her up and build up her confidence. You see, she'd been damn near killed in a car accident, and it had taken her months of physical therapy and a whole series of operations to be able to walk again."

"So that's why she referred to herself as a cripple," Char said. "How tragic."

"She's *not* a cripple!" Keith clenched his fist. "Not physically, anyway. By now, the only lasting *physical* effect of the accident is a slight limp the doctors say she'll have for the rest of her life. Unfortunately, she's obsessed by that limp. She's convinced that people see her as some kind of freak, so she's dropped most of her circle of friends and given up all attempts at a social life. It's heartbreaking for her parents, because Debbie was always such a pretty, vivacious, popular girl."

"So what did you do?" Despite her earlier antagonism, she'd become so caught up in his story that she forgot to feel awkward wearing just a towel.

"I tried to help, of course. I talked to her in a friendly, brotherly way, and took her out a few times to encourage her to get back into the swing of things. She's a nice girl, and I admired her for her courage and determination during all those months when she was struggling to walk again. But I never felt any romantic interest in her. I never even kissed her, except once on the cheek. How was I to guess she'd decided to fall madly in love with me?"

Char stared in disbelief at his disgruntled but still gorgeous face. The man was so handsome that most women probably went weak at the knees every time he smiled. Even she, who prided herself on being a competent, mature woman in control of her life, had trouble keeping her cool around him. In her opinion, unleashing the impossibly charming, sexy smiles of an "older man" like Keith Webb on a vulnerable, inexperienced teenager was like shouting "Fire!" in a crowded theater.

"Any fool could have predicted she would fall for you like a ton of bricks, Keith," she said wryly.

"Then I must be very dumb, because I had no idea. Not until four months ago, just after I returned from a short business trip to Chicago. That's when a few chance remarks from my aunt and uncle woke me up to the fact that people in Webb Falls were taking my 'relationship' with Debbie way too seriously. In their minds, I was practically engaged to her! After that, it didn't take me long to notice that Debbie herself had a king-size crush on me."

"Very observant of you."

"Don't rub it in. It was awful. I knew I had to stop seeing her, and I knew she'd be hurt. But the worst part was, she'd just found out her limp was going to be permanent. So whatever reasons I gave for not seeing her anymore, I knew she was bound to assume it was really because of *that*, even though it had nothing to do with it!"

Char sighed. "She told me that you could never love her because she was a cripple. That *nobody* could."

"Damn! That's the whole reason I lied to her in the first place—so she wouldn't torture herself with that kind of crazy reasoning. I didn't want to add any more emotional scars to hold her back from getting on with the rest of her life."

"So what did you tell her?"

"That there was another woman." His voice sounded hoarse and strained. He jammed his hands in his jeans pockets and swung around to start pacing back and forth across the floor. "I told her I'd just met this woman in Chicago and it had been love at first sight. An attraction so swift and powerful I couldn't help myself. This woman was the love of my life, I told Debbie."

"And what did Debbie say to that?" Char asked gently.

He stopped pacing, and the look in his eyes was the look of a man reliving a nightmare. "She just stood there staring up at me, turning white as paper and trying to blink back the tears. I felt like a monster. And then she said, 'I don't believe you. You're making this up, so you won't have to admit you don't want me because I'm a cripple.' "

"Oh, God," Char said brokenly.

"And then she said, 'I bet this perfect woman of yours doesn't even have a name, does she? Because she doesn't exist!' And then *I* said the first words that popped into my head. 'Of course she exists,' I said. 'And her name is Charlotte Smith.' "

Three

"*What*?" For the first time in all her twenty-nine years, Char thought she might faint.

"Forgive me. Until today, I honestly thought it was just a name I'd plucked out of thin air. But now I realize my memory was playing tricks on me. Your name must have been lurking in my brain because I'd read it on your résumé the week before."

"I don't believe this!" Her knees felt numb, so she sank down on the bed, never taking her eyes off Keith.

He moved across the room and sat down beside her. "Neither do I," he said with a gusty sigh. "I mean, what are the odds that the name I picked for the imaginary love of my life would turn out to belong to a living, breathing, flesh-and-blood woman who was destined to walk into my world four months later?" His eyes met hers, and then dropped to her bare shoulders and the damp towel that clung to the top of her breasts. "And that she would turn out to be so beautiful," he added softly.

Oh, dear. "Don't start trying to sweet-talk me,"

she warned, doing her best to ignore the prickles of awareness that chased up and down her flesh. "What you're saying is that there is no 'other' Charlotte Smith, right?"

"Right," he admitted glumly. "You're it, Char."

"And that means that Debbie, along with half of Webb Falls, thinks that you and I are one hot item. Right?"

"Wrong. *All* of Webb Falls thinks that, not just half."

"Terrific." She was going to have a lot of awkward explaining to do in the next three weeks. And Keith Webb deserved to be boiled in oil, long eyelashes and all, for landing her in this embarrassing situation! Even though he'd done it by accident, and with the best of intentions.

"I'm sorry, Char. It's unfair that an innocent bystander like you should get dragged into a mess like this. On the other hand . . ."

"On the other hand," she said philosophically, "it does have its humorous side. When I *think* of the look on your face when I walked into your office! No wonder you snarled at me like a treed wildcat! You knew right away the jig was up."

"Is it, Char?" His voice was so low and rough-edged with uncertainty that she could scarcely believe she'd heard him, except that his words seemed to echo again and again in her brain.

"What do you mean? As soon as Debbie finds out that you and I never met before today—"

His gaze locked with hers. "She doesn't have to find that out, Char."

"Don't be silly. Of course she—" She stopped in mid-sentence and stared into his jade-green eyes. Surely he couldn't be suggesting . . . "Oh, no!" she exclaimed, leaping up off the bed so fast she almost lost her towel. "Please say you're not asking *me* to pretend to be that woman you met in Chicago?"

The brief interval of silence before he spoke seemed to last an eternity. "I'm not just asking—I'm *begging*. For the sake of a nineteen-year-old kid who needs to stop feeling sorry for herself over a minor physical handicap that's scarcely noticeable to anyone but her."

Now it was Char's turn to pace back and forth across the room, trying to sort out the contradictory impulses she was feeling. Getting involved with a client in a tangled web of deception would be a very unwise, unprofessional thing to do. Especially when the client was a green-eyed heartbreaker like Keith Webb. But what about poor Debbie?

"How is my taking part in some silly charade going to help her?" she challenged him. "Wouldn't she be better off hearing the truth? It's a fact of life that the love we give isn't always returned, whether we walk with a limp or not. And learning that is part of growing up." She shook her head sadly. "I think you should have been honest with her in the first place."

"I know that now," he said bleakly. His elbows rested on his knees, and his knuckles cradled his hard jaw as he stared at the floor. "I made a mistake. But now it's too late."

"Why?"

"Don't you see? If she finds out *now* that I lied about my involvement with you, she'll feel I've made a fool of her—humiliated her—in front of everybody she knows," he said grimly. "And no matter what I say, she'll think she was right all along about why I quit seeing her! She'll withdraw deeper into her shell, until life can't reach her anymore. Is that what you want?"

"That's not fair, Keith! You got yourself into this mess, but now you're trying to make *me* feel guilty." And he was doing a pretty darn good job of it, too. She felt awful. "Oh, I'm so confused! Wouldn't it be simpler if you just made everybody happy by falling in love with Debbie after all?" *Except it wouldn't make me happy,* she realized.

"No, it wouldn't be *simple*," he said fiercely. "Fond as I am of Debbie, I just don't feel that special spark that a man should feel for his mate, his lover, his life's companion. It's not just because she's so young and we have so little in common. It's because of a multitude of small things, which end up meaning a lot. Like the fact that she never gets my jokes, that we don't laugh at the same things. What you're suggesting is impossible. And now more than ever." He broke off abruptly and glared at her.

"Sorry I asked," she said weakly, shaken by the passionate conviction of his words. Who would have guessed that Keith Webb's feelings about love would be so strong and, dared she think it, romantic?

His expression quickly changed to one of sheepish apology. "I told you I was a little touchy on that subject."

"A *lot* touchy," she reminded him, and somehow that made them both start to laugh. The tension between them, which had been building since Debbie's phone call, now slackened. Char slowed her nervous pacing, and allowed a whimsical thought to slip into her unwary brain: just supposing that she agreed to Keith's request, they might laugh together like this many times in the next three weeks. The thought triggered a warm glow inside her. Too warm. She frowned.

"I don't blame you for having reservations about this," Keith said sadly. "Any sane woman would think twice before getting tangled up in the affairs of a man she scarcely knows."

Char wasn't so sure that was true, at least not in

his case. Most of the sane women she knew would have leaped to become entangled in *his* affairs. So why wasn't she doing the same? "What concerns me is how it might look professionally," she admitted.

"What do you mean?"

"Well, you're my client. And if I'm supposed to have known you four months ago, *before* I was awarded the contract with your company, some people might get the idea that . . ." Her voice trailed off as she let him figure out the implications for himself.

"You're afraid they might think you got the contract because of our supposed relationship?"

She nodded.

"But that's absurd! The decision on the contract was made by one of my special task forces several days *before* my trip to Chicago. So there's no problem, right?" His disarming smile made her want to agree, although she knew there were still *lots* of problems.

"But, Keith," she managed to protest. "You *are* my client. That means I really shouldn't have any personal involvement with you at all!"

"Not any? Not even that kiss we shared out by the barn?" His green eyes teased her. "You knew when I kissed you that I was your client, so why didn't you stop me?"

Oh, dear. Why *hadn't* she stopped him? No answer occurred to her, at least none that she cared to mention to Keith. Her cheeks turned fire-engine red, and she refused to look him in the eye.

"I respect your professional ethics." To her surprise, he sounded as if he meant it. "But shouldn't there be a little room for compromise, under the circumstances? A young woman's happiness is at stake here."

"I know."

"Then help me, Char. And I promise I'll keep your involvement in this to a minimum."

"Just how do you plan on doing that?" She knew she sounded a bit hard and uncaring, but she'd learned long ago not to put much faith in men's promises. Her father, who'd left home for good when Char was eight years old, had been a great one for making wonderful promises. Too bad he'd never bothered to keep any of them.

"It shouldn't be difficult. After all, you'll only be in town for three weeks, right?"

"Yes, but . . ." A lot of involvement could happen in three weeks, she thought.

"And there's only one occasion when I'll really need your help. That's at the annual Webb Falls Community Dinner-Dance next weekend. Debbie has been saying for weeks that if I don't bring Charlotte to this dance it will prove she doesn't exist. And for weeks I've been making excuses about why you couldn't be there. But now . . ."

Oh, dear. He looked so hopeful. And those intent eyes of his and that deep, throaty voice were dangerously persuasive.

"That's all you need from me?" she asked hesitantly. "One public appearance with you at a local dance?" It didn't sound like so much, after all. It would hardly even count as "getting involved with a client," would it?

"That should be all. You'll be able to keep a pretty low profile. Though it might be a good idea for us to spend *some* time together during the rest of your stay in Webb Falls. Just enough so nobody gets suspicious," he added hastily.

"Mmm." Char scarcely heard him, because she was pacing again. Back and forth, she strode across the room, while her sensible, rational side tried to catch up with the part of her that had already reached a decision.

"What do you say, Char? Will you do it?"

She turned to face him.

"*Char?*" He said in a strangled voice. His face went pale beneath its tan, and his eyes suddenly blazed like neon. "Your . . . um . . ."

That did it. How could she say no to a man who got so choked up with emotion waiting for her to answer that he could scarcely speak?

"I'll do it," she announced.

Keith didn't seem to have heard. He just went on staring at her with a dazed, peculiar smile on his face.

"Keith?"

"Mmm?"

"I said, 'I'll do it.' "

"That's nice," he said absently.

"Nice? Is that all the thanks I get? I thought you'd be *pleased*."

"*You* would please any man, Char." A dreamy little smile played on his lips. "I don't know when I've ever been so . . . pleased. But I really should tell you, shouldn't I?"

"Tell me what?"

"Um . . . your towel . . ."

"My . . . towel?" She glanced down, and uttered a high-pitched gasp. "*My towel!*"

"It slipped," Keith pointed out helpfully.

"So I see." It was hard to miss, since the towel had slid practically to her navel! Blushing with mortification, Char tugged it back into place. "Listen, weren't you going to find me some clothes?" she demanded in a flustered voice.

"Coming right up." Grinning, he stooped to pick up the bundle of clothing he'd dropped when he first came in. "Here." He tossed her a pair of women's jeans and a plaid cotton shirt. "I borrowed these from my manager's wife."

"Thanks." Now, if only he'd leave so she could get dressed.

"Am I forgiven, Char?"

"What for?"

"For watching your towel slip." He sounded completely unrepentant.

"*No*, you're not forgiven! Dammit, Keith! You could have said something about that towel a lot sooner."

"I might have," he agreed with a wicked grin. "If I hadn't been enjoying the view so much."

The slow, deliberate way he said it set all her pulses throbbing like jungle drums. The man certainly had a talent for sounding blatantly seductive, Char thought distrustfully. It wasn't a trait she particularly admired. In fact, quite the opposite. So why was she letting him have this effect on her?

"I hope it's a view you don't plan on seeing again, Mr. Webb. Because I can tell you right now, you don't have the chance of a snowball in hell."

His disbelieving smile was so warm, she could have toasted marshmallows on it. "But I'll still have my memories, Char. And what memories they are!" he murmured teasingly.

Oh, dear. The look in his eyes told her he was remembering every vulnerable inch of her, right this minute.

"In fact," he went on, "what would you say if I told you I had a photographic memory?"

She couldn't blush any redder than she already was, so she just glared at him. "I'd say baloney. If you've got such a great memory, why didn't you remember that you'd seen my name on my résumé, instead of assuming you'd invented it yourself?"

His smile turned whimsical. "That's one more mystery I'm chalking up to fate."

"What's *that* supposed to mean?"

"I told you before, it was fate that brought us together like this, Char. My memory lapse must have been just one more strand in the web of destiny."

Char's jaw dropped open. Was he serious? No, of course not! And what kind of gullible fool did he take her for, anyway? Did he think he could dangle that kind of obvious line and then expect her to swallow it, hook, line, and sinker?

"Let's get one thing straight," she said indignantly. "Your phony sweet-talk may be a big hit with some women, but I don't happen to like it. And I may have agreed to pose as your girlfriend, but that's all I've agreed to. Don't expect any fringe benefits."

"Phony sweet-talk? Fringe benefits?" he roared, jumping up off the bed and glaring at her. "What the hell kind of guy do you think I am?"

"I don't *know* what kind of guy you are. We're still practically strangers, Keith."

Her quiet statement seemed to drain the anger from his body. "Oh. That's true." He frowned and looked surprised. "I guess I forgot." His look turned playful. "But for your information, I'm a *sweetheart* of a guy."

"I'm sure you are, but—"

"And my sweet-talk is *not* phony."

Char hesitated. "Listen, I'm sorry if I offended you. But I meant what I said. I'll pretend to be your woman from Chicago, for Debbie's sake, but don't try to take advantage of the situation, or of me. Because I won't tolerate it. Your company has hired me as its consultant, and that means there can't be any romantic involvement between us."

"Can't be?"

"Won't be."

"Fair enough." He shoved his hands in the

pockets of his jeans. "But just remember, I meant what *I* said too."

Char frowned at his broad back in mute frustration as he sauntered to the door.

"Come downstairs as soon as you're dressed," he said over his shoulder as he left the room. "We need to make plans about how to pull off this little charade."

The tiles of the kitchen floor felt cool and smooth beneath Char's bare feet. She took another bracing sip of the hot, strong coffee Keith had poured for her, and frowned at him across the gleaming oak of the kitchen table.

"This isn't going to work," she said.

"Why shouldn't it work?"

"Because the truth is, I couldn't act my way out of a paper bag! I'll never be able to convince Debbie that I'm the love of your life. I don't know what possessed me to say I would even try!"

"But, Char. You've already got *me* convinced. Why should it be so tough to convince Debbie?"

Her heart did a quick somersault before she reminded herself of what she already knew—that Keith Webb was a pro at making charming, lover-like speeches that meant absolutely nothing. How *could* they mean anything? He'd met her less than three hours ago, and she had it from his own mouth that she wasn't even his type.

The fact was, the man could turn his glib, sexy charm on and off like a water faucet, and now he'd chosen to turn it on her, because he needed her help. He was obviously well accustomed to using that charm and his stunning good looks to get what he wanted. Just the way her father had done, she thought in distaste.

Char sighed. She'd already told Keith she didn't

like it when he talked that way. That hadn't stopped him. Maybe she should just ignore his suggestive remarks. If she *could*. It was hard to ignore words spoken through chiseled, sensual lips—lips that often curved into a beguiling, mischievous smile. As they did now.

"Char?"

"What?"

"You're staring at my nose again."

"No, your lips. I mean . . . *no*, I'm not!"

"Whatever you say."

"I was staring into empty space—"

"My head is *not* empty space, dear lady."

"I didn't *notice* where I was staring! Because I was wracking my brain trying to figure out how you talked me into going along with this crazy, hopeless scheme!"

"Simple. I just appealed to the warmhearted, compassionate, caring woman I saw lurking beneath your brisk, businesslike exterior. And while my plan may be a little crazy, it's certainly not hopeless. There's no doubt in my mind that we'll convince Debbie and everyone else that we're madly in love."

"How?"

"Like this." He lifted her slender fingers to his lips and kissed them. Lingeringly. Reverently. Expertly. Char's whole arm was tingling as she tried to tug her hand away.

"What do you think you're doing?" she demanded.

"Kissing . . . your . . . wrist," he murmured breathlessly, as his lips moved across her palm to press against the throbbing blue veins of her wrist. She felt the hard wetness of his tongue flick against her pulse. Oh, dear.

"Well, stop it!" she cried.

He stopped, but didn't release her hand. "You're trembling."

"So?"

He smiled mysteriously. "And your eyes are shimmering."

She turned her face away. "Big deal."

"And now you're turning a lovely shade of pink," he said. "Don't you see, Char? You're acting just like a woman in love."

"But I'm not!"

"You and I know that. But nobody else would ever guess. So you've got nothing to worry about. Pretending to be in love with me will be a piece of cake."

"Arrogant swine," she muttered under her breath.

"What was that, Char?"

"Um . . . nothing. I just said, 'So everything's fine.' "

"That's the spirit! And don't worry that the burden will fall entirely on you," Keith said reassuringly. "I'll do my part. People will notice the dreamy look in my eyes when I'm with you. They'll see the way I turn my head to catch the sound of your voice, even when you're clear across the room. They'll see that I can't keep my hands off you, that—"

"Keith!"

"Yes?"

"Surely all that won't be necessary. Can't we just—"

"Of course it's necessary. But I promise you, it'll all come naturally. Easy as pie."

Char hoped it didn't come *too* naturally. The last thing she needed was to fall for Keith's bewitching but insincere charm. She dropped her worried gaze to her left hand, noting with surprise that it still lay meekly and contentedly in Keith's grasp.

Her eyes traced the taut curve of his fingers where they encircled her wrist. Following the corded ridges of his tendons along the back of his hand, her gaze climbed to his tanned, muscled forearm. He had gorgeous forearms, she decided, contemplating the hard layering of muscle encased in skin like golden brown silk, lightly sprinkled with crisp dark hair. The muscles strained against the faded blue cotton of his rolled-up shirtsleeves.

"Char?"

"Mmm?"

"What are you staring at *now*?"

"Your shirtsleeves. Has anyone told you, you've got a great pair of shirtsleeves?" Oh, dear. Had she actually said that? Char yanked her gaze away to stare fixedly into her coffee cup, wishing she could dive into its murky depths and disappear.

"Nope. You're the first." He began silkily stroking her wrist with his thumb. "How about my shirt collar? What's your opinion of *it*?"

She managed a swift, nervous glance upward at the open neck of his shirt, and hastily looked down again. Keith's smooth, tanned throat was every bit as gorgeous as his forearms were. And the caress of his thumb on her captive wrist was sending unsettling vibrations all through her body.

"Well?" he prompted.

"Your collar is fine too. Though it's a bit frayed," she added truthfully.

"It's an old shirt," he said in agreement, shrugging slightly. Out of the corner of her eye, Char caught the easy, rippling motion of his shoulder muscles, and shivered. "But I'm glad you like it. Now, what about my eyes?"

"Your eyes?"

"I'd like your opinion of them."

"Well, um . . ." She was afraid to look at him. Afraid to meet the electric, compelling current of desire that sparked in those eyes of his. She stared blindly into her coffee cup. "They're green," she said.

"Yes, I know. But what do you think of them?"

She refused to lift her gaze. "They're very nice."

"Are you sure? Don't you think you should take another look, to refresh your memory? Just so there's no mistake."

"I don't usually make mistakes. Tell me, is this a trick to get me to look at you?"

"Well, yes."

"Why?"

"If you look at me, I'll tell you why."

"Oh, what the heck!" She tilted her chin up at him defiantly. "Tell me, then."

That *was* a mistake. His kiss was swift, devastating, inevitable. His hands cupped her face, and his lips descended over her mouth with hungry, demanding passion.

Her heart thudded with excitement even as she tried to pull away from him. No other man had ever had this power to kindle her so rapidly to arousal, with only the touch of his hand on hers and his kiss on her lips. But then, no other man's kiss had ever felt like this.

The pressure of his tongue against her lips was so sweetly sensual, she couldn't bear not to surrender to it. Slowly her lips parted. Rhythmically, irresistibly, his tongue probed her mouth, exploring its silken pink depths. Char felt the pleasure of his lightest touch flowing through her, blotting out everything except the craving for more.

And he gave her more. His hands played in her hair, pulling at the pins that kept it coiled so neatly against her neck. His voice whispered soft words in her ear as his fingers combed through the long, satiny waves of auburn hair that tumbled down around her shoulders. He kissed her mouth again and then her white throat as he undid the top two buttons of her shirt.

Then, without warning, his seeking hands and lips grew still. He buried his face in the curve of her neck for a long moment, breathing hard.

"Damn. I'm sorry," he said.

Four

"*You're* sorry?" Char gave a tremulous laugh. She was the one who was sorry. How could she have let him kiss her again? She'd had every reason not to, starting with their professional relationship as consultant and client. And of course she'd known what he was up to.

"Hell, yes, I'm sorry!" he said, abruptly leaning back in his chair. "I had no business doing that, after you'd explained your feelings about becoming personally involved with a client. I never meant to stampede you into doing something you'd feel ashamed of, Char."

She stared at him in confusion. "Then why did you?"

"Would you believe I couldn't help myself?"

"*No.*"

"You're right." He smiled ruefully. "Kissing you just now was damn near irresistible, but that's no excuse. What can I say? I'll just have to try harder to behave myself around you."

"See that you do." Somehow she managed to disguise the tremor in her voice. If he *didn't* behave himself, she was going to have the devil's own time behaving *herself*. And that was a very scary thought.

"Don't look so worried," he said. "If I really set my mind to it, I'm sure I can handle a little temptation." His gaze lingered on her red, kiss-swollen mouth and then dipped to the unbuttoned neckline of her borrowed shirt. He swallowed. "Maybe even a *lot* of temptation."

Hastily Char refastened the two buttons Keith had so recently undone. " 'Maybe' isn't good enough," she said. "After all, you *promised*, when I agreed to help you, that my involvement would be kept to a minimum. But your kisses are *not* minimal."

"It's a relief to hear you say that!" The teasing light was back in his eyes.

She responded with a lethal glance. "What about your promise?" she asked. "Can you keep it?"

His expression grew serious. "I'll have to, won't I? You're sticking your neck out to help me, so it's only fair for me to respect your wishes concerning our relationship."

It sounded so simple, when he put it like that. But Char had a feeling it wasn't going to be simple at all. Her premonition deepened with his next words.

"I did promise that you'd be involved as little as possible, and I intend to keep my word. But I can't make the same promise about my own involvement, Char."

"I wouldn't expect you to," she said nervously. "After all, this is your town, Debbie is someone you've known all your life, and this whole thing is *your* problem. It's only natural for you to feel very deeply involved."

"That's not what I meant, and you know it. I was talking about my involvement with *you*."

Oh, dear. "Well, *don't*. Don't talk about it," she pleaded. "I'm sure it's just a figment of your imagination."

"You think so?" His voice and expression gave no clue as to whether he was offended or amused by her remark. "We'll just have to wait and see, won't we?"

Keith eased his foot off the accelerator of the sporty two-seater maroon Mercedes as it cruised into the outskirts of Webb Falls.

"I still say the pickup truck has more character," Char said, continuing the on-again, off-again debate that had sprung up when Keith relegated the muddy pickup to the garage and assisted Char into this sleek, elegant automobile. Even the contented purr of its engine spoke of wealth and power.

"You're mistaking mud for character," Keith insisted. "The truck is great around the farm, but *this* is the car to have for squiring around a beautiful woman. Come on, admit it—you love this car."

"All right, I love it." What else could she say? She did love it. The rich softness of the leather upholstery was pure luxury against her body, and the sensation of smooth, responsive speed was exhilarating.

"Good. And now admit that you'd love to have dinner with me tonight."

"Keith, I already said no. Twice. And the last time was only five minutes ago."

"I was hoping you might have changed your mind since then."

"Nope. And I'm not going to, so you can quit asking. I want to keep a low profile here in Webb Falls, remember?"

"But, Char, how will people believe we're in love if

I let you eat dinner alone on your first night in town?"

"Nobody will know. I'll buy some bread, cheese, fruit, and yogurt at a grocery store, and then eat in my motel room."

"Ugh. That sounds dreary and depressing."

"It sounds nice and peaceful to me. I've had enough excitement for one day."

He gave her a sidelong smile. "So you find me exciting, do you?"

"I find you conceited beyond belief."

Keith laughed. "Which motel are you staying at?"

Char hesitated. She wanted to say, "None of your business." After all, the last thing she needed was for this distractingly handsome hunk to show up for a cozy visit in some tiny motel room that was eighty percent bed. For a fast worker like him, it wouldn't even be a challenge.

"You might as well tell me. Since there are only two motels in all of Webb Falls, it shouldn't take me long to track you down anyway."

She conceded with a sigh. "The Wayside."

He nodded. "Room number?"

The *nerve* of him! "I have no idea." Her voice practically dripped icicles. "I haven't even checked in yet. I've got a reservation, so I assume they'll hold a room for me at least till six." She glanced at her watch. "It's only four now."

"You shouldn't have any trouble. The motel business isn't exactly booming in Webb Falls on a Monday night."

"Good. I left my car at the plant, so I'd appreciate it if you'd just drop me off there."

"Char . . ."

"What?"

"Please stop this."

"Stop what?"

"Trying to pretend we're strangers. We're not, you know. Not anymore. We've known each other three whole hours! I've helped you out of a mud puddle, I've kissed you twice, I've thrown myself on your mercy, I've seen you with your hair down, not to mention with your *towel* down—"

"Darn you, Keith Webb! Don't *remind* me!"

"Then don't pretend it never happened."

"I wish it never had." But that wasn't quite true, and she knew it. Oh, not the part about her towel slipping. She wanted to die of embarrassment every time she remembered *that*. But the rest of their three hours together had felt so . . . special. *She* had felt special. So alive. So warm and womanly and witty and desirable, all at the same time. No man had ever made her feel that way before. But maybe that was only because she'd never known a man who'd had so much *practice* at making women feel special, she thought sadly. Keith was too awesomely good at it to be believed.

He took a quick look at her face, and bit off a curse. "Damn. Please stop looking so sad, beautiful Char," he pleaded. "I promise, you're going to be glad our lives collided like this. Just trust me."

But *could* she trust him? Char didn't think so, and that was why she looked even sadder than before as they pulled into the Webb Company parking garage.

After so many months of doing consulting work in one city after another, Char was adept at finding her way around a new town. And Webb Falls was easier to deal with than most. By a quarter to five that afternoon, she'd already checked into the Wayside Motel, changed out of her borrowed jeans into pale gray pleated slacks and a melon-colored knit top, and located the only dry cleaner's shop in town.

The plump little man behind the counter at the cleaner's let out a long, low whistle when he saw the mud stains on the suit Char handed him. "You must have taken a heck of a tumble!" he exclaimed.

"Um . . . yes, I tripped and fell in some mud," Char said with a polite smile. She wasn't used to dry cleaners who took a personal interest in the spots and stains on their customers' clothes.

"I suppose it happened out at the old Tucker place?"

Char stared at him in total bafflement.

"The farm that young Keith Webb bought when Mel Tucker retired last year," he added by way of explanation.

"Oh!" *How did he know?* "Um, yes, that is where it happened, as a matter of fact."

"Thought so." He grunted in satisfaction. "Mrs. Reardon said she saw young Keith and a red-headed gal she'd never set eyes on before, heading out that way in his pickup this afternoon. And Cissy Gaines, that works at the Webb plant, came by on her coffee break to pick up her party dress for next Saturday, and she said the whole plant was buzzing because the boss's lady had showed up."

Oh, dear. So much for keeping a low profile.

The man pursed his lips and cocked his bushy gray eyebrows assessingly at Char. "So you're the foxy lady from Chicago that's set the Webb boy's heart all aflame and aflutter."

Char gulped, barely controlling her impulse to deny everything.

"Don't worry," he said. "*I* don't fault you for it, though there's some that might. But I never did think little Debbie Forrest was the gal for him. No, he needs a bit more pepper and spice, and I can see you're just the one to give it to him."

She tried to speak, couldn't, and instead made a helpless gesture toward her mud-stained suit lying on the counter.

"Oh, sure, young lady, I'll have that cleaned up for you, good as new, by the end of the week."

"Thank you," Char said in a strangled voice.

"Name?" he asked, holding a pen poised over the top half of the claim check for her suit.

"Smith. First initial C."

"C for Charlotte, right?"

"Right." Why had he even bothered to ask? she wondered. No doubt his network of spies had already told him everything there was to know about her.

"Phone number?"

"Um . . . whatever the number is at the Wayside Motel."

Without stopping to look it up, he penned in a number, and Char marveled at his amazing memory for small details. He seemed to consume, store, and regurgitate information more effectively than a computer. But that reminded her of another man who claimed to have a phenomenal memory— Keith.

Keith was bound to show up at her motel room that night. She just knew it. He'd smile that lazy, sensual smile that would tell her he was remembering the heated abandon of her kisses and the way she looked with her towel half gone. And there'd be no place to retreat to—not in her miniscule room at the Wayside, which, just as she'd feared, was wall-to-wall bed.

"Tell me," she said, trying to hide the desperation in her voice, "do you know of any place in town where I could rent a room for the next three weeks? Something a little more . . . homey than a motel?" The man behind the counter seemed to know everything else going on in Webb Falls, she reasoned, so why not that?

"Funny you should ask. Just yesterday, Mrs. Benson was saying to me how the sweet old lady she's had boarding with her for the last three years has moved to Rochester to live with her daughter. In my opinion, you couldn't find a nicer place to stay than Faye Benson's."

"But would she be willing to rent to a stranger, and for only three weeks?" Char asked doubtfully.

He laughed. "Don't forget you've got the most important man in town to vouch for you, young lady."

"I do?" It took her a second to realize he meant Keith. "Oh, right," she said, blushing.

"Besides . . ." He lowered his voice confidingly. "Don't let on I said anything, but Faye really needs the money. She's had a time of it since her husband passed away and left her a stack of hospital bills and three kids to raise. And now her son Steve's at the university, studying to be a doctor. Of course Faye is tickled pink that he's doing so well, but a college education don't come cheap."

"No. No, it doesn't," Char said sympathetically. She thought of her own mother, who'd also been 'left' with three kids to raise. "Can you give me Mrs. Benson's address?"

He hesitated. "I should mention, she's a mite old-fashioned about some things. She won't want you entertaining young Keith up in your room, you understand."

"I understand." Char almost beamed with gleeful relief. A strict dragon of a landlady was just what she needed to protect her from her own dangerous weakness when it came to Keith Webb. "Her place sounds *ideal*."

He wrote the address on a slip of paper and handed it to her. "You can't miss it. The big yellow house on the corner of Maple and Vine. The one that needs a paint job."

"Thank you for your help, Mr. . . . ."

"Schwartz. But just call me Lester."

He *looked* like a Lester, she decided. But as she thanked him again and set off for Mrs. Benson's, she was thinking that Lester Schwartz might be an angel in disguise. Because Mrs. Benson's house sounded like the perfect place for her to stay during the next three weeks.

Lester gave a satisfied smile as he watched Char's tall, slim figure stride away. He was congratulating himself on once again bringing together two people who needed each other—Faye needed a boarder, and the young lady needed a room.

"Good work, Lester," he said proudly. But suddenly a frown puckered his bushy eyebrows. He'd just remembered a reason—no, make that three reasons!—why it might be a mistake for Keith Webb's foxy lady friend to stay at the Benson place.

He hurried to the door of his shop, hoping to call her back. But she was already two blocks away, turning the corner onto Vine Street.

Lester shrugged. It was too late to stop her. As he stood staring down the street, a most unangelic grin split his wrinkled face. "Wish I could be a fly on the wall when those Benson kids find out who their mom's rented a room to. There's sure to be mischief." He chuckled to himself as he closed the shop for the night.

Char was feeling slightly smug that evening when the knock came on her motel-room door. No matter what fancy moves Keith Webb tried to pull tonight, she was confident she could keep things under control. And by this time tomorrow she'd be safely moved into her room at Faye Benson's. A lovely room with delicately sprigged wallpaper, white lace curtains at the bay windows, and a carved antique rocker. Not to mention geraniums growing in pots on the windowsill. She sighed blissfully.

The knock was repeated, more loudly this time. Char stepped to the window and parted the avocado-green drapes. All her hunches were right on target, she saw. Keith looked bigger and sexier and handsomer than ever as he stood on her doorstep, scowling impatiently. Her heartbeat slammed into high gear as she opened the door.

Without waiting for an invitation, Keith stepped inside, thrusting a brown paper bag into her hands. "Milk and cookies," he said gruffly.

"Milk and cookies?"

"Chocolate chip. Homemade an hour ago by Maggie, my manager's wife. The lady who lent you the jeans, remember? I knew you'd need something more substantial than fruit and yogurt."

She handed the bag back to him. "Thanks, but—"

Wordlessly he opened the bag and let the rich, chocolaty aroma of freshly baked cookies swirl up into her nostrils.

Char closed her eyes. "Well, maybe just one . . ."

"Now you're talking," he murmured, and dropped a warm, sweet, cookie-flavored kiss on her parted lips.

Her eyes flew open in shock, and she pulled away from him. "You know I didn't mean— For heaven's sake! I was talking about *cookies*!"

"My mistake," he apologized in velvety tones of phony regret, while his laughing eyes caressed her face as if it had been days instead of hours since their last meeting. "You look beautiful tonight," he whispered.

She blushed in confusion. Oh, dear. He was trying to sweet-talk her again. And she'd almost fallen for it.

"Thanks for the cookies, but I think you'd better leave."

His face drooped into comical lines of exaggerated disappointment. "You don't want to share them? I was *so* looking forward to—"

She shoved the bag at him. "Here, take them! And don't pretend you haven't already helped yourself to a few, because I tasted cookie on your lips when—"

"When I kissed you," Keith said helpfully.

"Right."

"I love it when you blush like this, Char. It's so damn sexy. First I say something, and then I see pink fire spreading over your face and down your neck. It makes me feel as if I'm touching you in all those places where you're blushing that I can't see."

Oh, dear. Char felt her flushed skin turn even warmer. "You mustn't say things like that!" Her voice sounded weak and trembly, even to her own ears.

"Mustn't I?"

"No! Our professional relationship—"

"Yes, I know." He sighed and pulled out a chair next to the small table that stood against the wall, under the window. "Sit down, and I'll get us some glasses for the milk."

She sank spinelessly onto the green vinyl chair and stared numbly after Keith as he went into the tiny bathroom. He returned immediately with the two paper-wrapped glasses that had been next to the sink.

"Dig in," he invited after unwrapping the glasses, pouring the milk, and setting the cookies out on a blue-and-white-checked cloth napkin. He lowered his long, muscular frame onto the other chair, which creaked beneath him.

Hesitantly Char reached out and took a cookie. Keith popped an entire one in his mouth and chewed it slowly, ecstatically. His long, dark lashes fanned across his hard, tanned cheekbones as he closed his eyes in delight. Char watched his throat muscles move in a series of ripples while he swallowed. His tongue shot out to lick the last crumb from his lips, and she shivered.

"Mmm, good," he said. His voice was sensual, and slow as molasses. Char took a quick, deep breath, and found herself choking on the cookie crumb she'd just sucked into her windpipe.

"Oh, help," she said, coughing and gasping.

"Char?" Instantly he was on his feet, leaning over her, pounding her on the back. "Do you need me to use the Heimlich maneuver?"

"No," she managed to gasp out. "I'm okay. It's unstuck." Her eyes were streaming and her throat felt sore, but she could breathe again.

Keith whipped a handkerchief out of his pocket and gently wiped her eyes. "Blow your nose," he ordered, and she did. His left hand was cradling her shoulders, and she relaxed against the comfort and reassurance of his touch. "Here, drink this, nice and slow." He held the glass of milk to her lips, and she obediently drank it.

The milk soothed her throat, and Char managed a wan smile. "Thanks," she said, embarrassed at causing such a fuss. She hadn't choked on a cookie since she was six years old, for crying out loud!

He breathed a loud sigh of relief. "You scared the hell out of me, Char! If I'd known what a chocolate-chip cookie could do to you, I'd never have brought them."

"Does that mean you won't let me have another one?"

He eyed her in consternation. "Do you really *want* another one?"

"Yes, please," she said meekly.

"Oh, all right. If you promise to be more careful this time."

"I promise."

Keith watched her like a hawk as she cautiously chewed and swallowed the cookie. Just when she'd begun to feel uneasy and self-conscious under his silent scrutiny, he spoke.

"I didn't come here just to risk your life by feeding you chocolate-chip cookies."

Char's throat felt suddenly dry, and she reached for the glass of milk. "Oh?"

"We need to talk some more, Char. Plan what we'll say when people ask how we met."

She breathed an inward sigh of relief. If all he wanted to do was *talk* . . . "Didn't you say we met in Chicago?" she asked.

"Chicago's a big town." He grinned. "And there're eight million stories in the naked city."

"Chicago's the *windy* city," she reminded him.

"Whatever. There are still eight million stories. And we'd better be sure that you and I tell everybody the same one."

"Good idea." She looked at him expectantly. "Well, you're the one with the overactive imagination. Do tell—how did we meet?"

His eyes grew dreamy. "We met . . . on a day in early spring. A playful breeze was chasing the sailboats on Lake Michigan. Fluffy clouds cast fitful shadows as they raced across the sun, making the air seem to move and sway like a field of pale yellow daffodils."

Char could practically feel the breeze and the warmth of that sun as he spoke. What a spellbinder he was with words, she thought. But that was an untrustworthy magic, as she knew from bitter experience.

"You, Char, were standing on the steps of the Art Institute," he continued. "Your hand was resting on one of the big stone lions that flank the entrance to the museum, and the wind was tugging at your hair, trying to pull it down around your shoulders. That's what caught my eye as I was jogging back to my hotel after a run along the lakefront—your hair, glowing like flame in the sunshine. And then I noticed how like a goddess you looked—tall and beautiful, with that tamed lion at your side."

"Keith . . ." she protested at his fanciful picture. But he went on as if he hadn't heard her speak.

"Then I saw you stroke the sun-warmed stone of the lion's side, as if you were petting a giant cat. That one small gesture warmed my heart, and sent an arrow of desire into my flesh. I wanted you. I wanted that woman who was so overflowing with a sensual, playful, affectionate love of life that she would caress a statue."

Char stared at him, almost believing that she *was* that woman he spoke of, that she had stood on those steps on that windy spring day, and that her hand had stroked that stone lion. She could picture Keith as he must have looked—his black hair tousled by the wind, his muscles molded by the knit fabric of his jogging suit, his face glowing from his run along the lake, and his green eyes blazing with desire. The image was so vivid that her pulse began to race.

"Just then," he said, "your gaze met mine. You guessed that I'd seen you pet the lion, and you blushed self-consciously. But you also laughed. Your laughing face was so warm and beautiful, it made my chest ache with wanting you. Like a man in a dream, I felt myself start up the steps toward you."

Her body tensed. "No," she said. It was almost a whimper of panic. How could she resist the vibrant sexual magnetism of the man closing in on her?

Keith's face grew somber. "Instantly your laughter stilled and your body went rigid. Your hand tightened on the leather portfolio you carried under your arm. You quickly turned to walk away, into the museum."

Char breathed a deep, audible sigh of relief. Or was it disappointment?

His resonant, evocative voice continued to spin its magic. "I stopped, halfway up the steps, overcome by a sudden, heartbreaking certainty; my flame-haired goddess wasn't the type who would ever, *ever*, let herself be picked up by a stranger on the steps of a museum."

"Never?"

"Never. Not even if all the planets had aligned to foretell our meeting. Not even if a whole choir of angels had burst into song right over our heads. Not even if you were turning your back on the best thing that could ever happen to both of us."

She stared at him, wide-eyed, scarcely able to breathe. How could it just end that way?

"But fate was on our side, Char. A miracle happened."

"It did?"

"Yes. Two children were playing tag on the steps of the Art Institute that day. One of them lost his balance and bumped into you, knocking the leather portfolio out of your hand. It fell, upside down, onto the steps. Papers spilled out. You gasped in horror as a gust of wind swirled them out of your reach. They flew away like a flock of white doves, alighting briefly on the sidewalk below. I was off like a flash, determined to save them for you."

"And did you?" But there was no need to ask. She knew he'd rescued every last one.

"Of course. I did have my running shoes on, you know."

"Of course. Silly me."

"And then comes the best part of all," he said. "Just as I caught up with the last sheet of paper and bent down to pick it up, a name seemed to leap off the page at me. 'Webb.' As in 'the Webb Company.' *My* company." He beamed. "I was holding a page from your notes on the proposal for the consulting assignment!"

"*What?*" she asked incredulously.

"After that, I introduced myself as your future client, and the rest was easy. Of course you had no qualms about getting better acquainted with me once you knew—"

"*Baloney!*" Char exploded, wanting her words to cut like shrapnel through the silken web of his impossible fabrications. "Nobody will buy this story! It's got more holes than a hunk of Swiss cheese."

"Baloney and Swiss cheese," Keith muttered mournfully. "I guess I should have brought you some sandwiches along with the cookies."

"Don't try to change the subject. I'm telling you, your story is totally improbable." She chose to ignore the fact that she'd been falling for it herself up until a minute ago. "It's got too many fantastical coincidences. What we need is a story that makes logical sense."

"It made perfect sense to me." Keith looked very disappointed. "What do you suggest?"

"We can't expect people to believe we met only by chance and *then* discovered our professional connection. *I* say we met because you wanted to discuss the consulting project with me once I'd been hired by your company."

"How . . . practical."

"I suppose you mean boring?"

"Well, I do like my story better. But if you insist . . . I phoned you in Chicago, and we agreed to meet over dinner."

Char contradicted him. "*Lunch.*"

"Right. At an intimate little bistro in the Loop. The weather was lousy—a freak spring snowstorm had blown in off the Lake. You were late, and I didn't like being kept waiting. But then . . . I looked up and saw you coming toward me. Snowflakes clung to your bright hair and melted against your flushed cheeks. Your eyes sparkled like a starry midnight sky. I knew right then that I'd be willing to wait for you forever. Even though you'd already kept me waiting my whole life."

"Keith . . ." she said falteringly.

"Mmm?"

"You're embellishing this too much. All we need to say is that we met, we . . . felt an attraction, and then . . ."

"Then, while the snow fell softly on the pavement outside and the gray afternoon light faded to dusk, you and I lingered over coffee and brandy, telling each other the stories of our lives. We couldn't take our eyes off each other. Each of us was thinking, 'I've found you at last.' "

"Oh, dear," Char whispered, closing her eyes under the weight of his hypnotic imagining.

"I've found you at last," he repeated huskily, and his voice sounded much nearer now. When Char opened her eyes in alarm, she saw that he'd moved his chair around the table, right next to hers.

She backed her chair away.

He inched his chair closer.

"Isn't this room hideous?" Char exclaimed feverishly. "That is, unless you're a big fan of avocado green?"

"Can't say that I am." He gave her a lecherous grin. "But the view from here is pretty nice." She couldn't decide whether his pointed stare was meant for her or for the bed right behind her. Either way, it made her nervous.

"Thank goodness I only have to put up with it for one night," she babbled.

"Huh?"

"Oh, didn't I tell you?" Of course, she knew darn well she *hadn't* told him. "I've rented a room from a woman here in town—a Mrs. Benson."

"Mrs. *who?*" He sounded aghast.

"Faye Benson. She seems like a very nice person, and the room is charming. It's in that big yellow house on—"

"I *know* where the Bensons live, Char," he growled impatiently. "Why the hell didn't you consult me before you went ahead with this?"

"Why the hell should I? Just because we're pretending to be in love doesn't mean I need your permission to rent a room!" She was on her feet, fists clenched at her sides, ready to launch into a full-scale shouting match if he persisted in coming on like a domineering, macho male.

It took her a second to realize that this particular domineering, macho male had slumped forward, his shoulders shaking with silent laughter. She ground her teeth and glared at him. "Care to share the joke?"

"Oh, damn, I shouldn't be laughing." He bit his lip and fixed her with a worried look that kept threatening to dissolve into renewed laughter. "We could be in big trouble, Char."

"Oh, really?" How big could the trouble be, she wondered, if he couldn't keep a straight face long enough to tell her about it?

"Yes, really. You know what you've gone and done, Char?"

"Of course. I've rented a lovely room in a beautiful old house, and I'm sure I'll be very comfortable there."

"Wrong. What you've just done is to stick your head into a hornets' nest."

"Huh?"

"You've set up your tent behind enemy lines."

"What tent? This isn't a camping trip!"

Keith looked down his nose at her. "I was speaking metaphorically."

"Well, please *don't*. Just get to the point. What have I done that's so terrible?"

"You've walked straight into the biggest cow pie in six counties."

"Now, hold on! If that's a slur on Faye Benson's housekeeping, I beg to differ! Why, that old place sparkles! The carpets may be worn, but the—"

"I'm not talking about Faye or her housekeeping—I'm talking about her *kids*! And especially her daughter Ann!"

Char stared at him in bewilderment. "Faye did mention that one of her daughters is a teenager, but so what? I don't mind subjecting my eardrums to an occasional Cyndi Lauper or Madonna tune."

Keith's smile was pitying. "Would you care to guess *who* is Ann Benson's very best friend in the whole world?"

It took her a moment, but then the answer plopped into her head with a heavy thud. "Not . . . Debbie?"

He nodded. "Debbie."

Five

Char's level gaze moved assessingly from face to face around the conference table. These three men and two women comprised the steering committee that had selected her to do the feasibility study that would shape personnel policy here at the Webb Company for years to come. She owed them, at the very least, her undivided attention.

After all, as a high-level consultant for the prestigious Boston firm of Brannon-Hale, her time did not come cheap. The Webb Company would be billed for every fraction of an hour she spent on this project. And they weren't paying her to think about last night in the motel room with Keith, she reminded herself crossly.

A quick glance at her neatly typed pages of notes reassured her. She was prepared for any preliminary questions the committee might have. Her previous experience with this type of study had been extensive, and she was sure she could handle any contingency. Any contingency, that is, except a silver-tongued hunk named Keith Webb.

Oh, dear, she was thinking about him *again.*

Frankly, it was hard not to. Especially now that she had *tonight* to worry about. Keith had convinced her she would have to go out with him this evening, all because she'd rented a room at the Bensons'. It seemed that with Ann, Steve, and Lisa Benson spying on her—and Keith had insisted that they *would* spy on her, and would report back to Debbie on every move she made—it was imperative that she spend more time with Keith. Or so Keith had said. And she had let him persuade her.

"Ms. Smith?"

"Uh, yes?" She jerked her concentration back to the present just in time to respond to a question about whether job-sharing wouldn't result in higher fringe-benefit costs to the company.

"There are several practical solutions to that problem," she explained. "Prorating, cost-sharing, 'cafeteria'-style benefits—" The words caught in her throat as Keith walked in. He looked just as sexy at nine A.M. as he'd looked some ten hours ago, when he'd kissed her a quick but memorable good night at her motel-room door . . . just in case anybody was watching, he'd said.

"Sorry for interrupting." A quick nod and a smile acknowledged the greetings of the committee members, and then his eyes rested with special warmth on Char. "I have an announcement to make."

What was he up to now? she wondered.

"Some of you may have heard rumors about my relationship with Ms. Smith, here. I'd like to set the record straight."

Oh, dear. Char's cheeks reddened as five pairs of eyes turned to regard her with lively curiosity.

"Ms. Smith and I met four months ago in Chicago, shortly after this committee's decision to award her the contract for the work she's about to undertake for us. I contacted her to discuss the project in greater detail. And then . . ." He paused, a little too melodramatically and suggestively, it seemed to Char. What were these people going to think?

"Then . . . I fell in love." He smiled in her direction, and she wanted to strangle him! Couldn't he see this was *not* the way for her to keep a low profile?

"But neither Ms. Smith nor I," he continued, "wants our personal feelings to interfere with her work here. That's why I'm delegating all responsibility for the project to this committee. You will oversee and evaluate Ms. Smith's work, and you will have the final say on whether her recommendations are accepted or rejected. No favoritism. Understood?"

He glanced swiftly around the table, collecting a unanimous show of startled nods. "Good." He beamed at Char. "Carry on, Ms. Smith, and I'll see you in my office after the meeting." He left the room with a jaunty, satisfied spring to his step.

Char gritted her teeth and prayed for strength before she lifted her head to meet the uneasy expressions of the committee members. They were eyeing her as if she'd just sprouted horns. *Damn and blast that man!* she thought.

"Um, as I was saying on the issue of fringe-benefit costs," she said. Her only hope now was to so thoroughly dazzle them with her competence that they'd forget the way Keith had just confirmed every piece of harmful gossip buzzing around the place. Thanks to him, the next half hour, if not the next three weeks, would likely turn out to be the most difficult she'd ever endured.

Thanks a hell of a lot, Webb. But she hid her angry, sarcastic thoughts under a businesslike smile, and proceeded to tell the committee members what they needed to know about balancing fringe-benefit costs.

"How could you do that to me?" Char had carefully refrained from slamming the door of Keith's office, and now she crossed to his desk in three brisk strides.

His welcoming smile turned to puzzlement. "What'd I do?"

"You and your damned 'announcement,' " she said bitterly. "If people weren't talking about us before, they will be now! I *told* you I wanted to keep a low profile on this."

"But, Char, all I did was explain things for the committee. I've always made it a policy to keep my employees informed, and I've found that being aboveboard with them leads to mutual trust and respect." He gave her a reassuring smile. "Now that they know exactly what the situation is, the talk will die down in no time."

Char was not reassured.

"You honestly believe that, don't you?" Her voice squeaked with incredulity. "You just poured gasoline on a raging bonfire of gossip and speculation, and you think the flames are about to *die down*?"

"What's there for people to talk about, now that they know the facts?" he asked in a reasonable tone.

"You obviously don't know much about people," she said bluntly. "And you seem to be forgetting something—those 'facts' you gave them aren't even true! We did *not* meet four months ago in Chicago, and you aren't in love with me."

"What makes you so sure?"

"Don't start *that* again," she said severely. But his soft-spoken words awakened a tremor of uncertainty inside her. She walked over to the expanse of window behind Keith's desk, and stared, unseeing, at the green-gold hills and dark-boughed woods that lay beyond the pane of glass.

Could there be a grain of truth at the bottom of all the impossibly romantic things he kept saying to her? she wondered. Oh, she knew he was physically attracted to her, but could there be something more? Something deeper? And if there was, how would she feel about it?

Scared out of her mind, she admitted wryly. But there was no point in thinking about that, since Keith couldn't possibly be sincere. He was simply the type of man who would come up with a "hearts and flowers" speech for any occasion, right on cue. Those amazing fairy tales he'd invented last night about their first meeting were a perfect example of that.

"Char?" he said hesitantly, stepping close to her at the window, studying the pensive lines of her face in profile. "I did what I thought would make your job easier. If it turns out it was the wrong approach, then I'm sorry, and I'll do my best to set it right again."

"Please. Don't do me any more favors." But she turned to him and smiled as she said it. It was true that Keith always seemed to act with the *best* of intentions. That's how he'd gotten them into this whole crazy mess in the first place.

"I should have talked it over with you first," he said ruefully. "Just the way *you* should have told me about your plans to rent a room at the Benson's. We conspirators have to learn to communicate better, Char."

His voice had deepened, and he moved closer—so close that Char could feel the warmth of his body, though they weren't quite touching. And his eyes were doing one heck of a job of communicating, she observed nervously. They radiated fire that

spoke of passion, yearning, and excitement. Everything she herself was feeling, she realized. Everything but the fear. There was no fear or doubt in
Keith's eyes. Only in her own.

"What time shall I pick you up for dinner
tonight?" he asked softly.

"Must we?" Char sighed.

"We must. The question is when."

"I'll need some time to get settled into my new
room. Would seven-thirty be too late?"

"Seven-thirty is fine. I'm looking forward to it."

"Well, *don't*. This date is just for show,
remember?"

"That won't stop me from finding pleasure in
your company, Char." Without warning, he
dropped a kiss on the tip of her nose, and that one
quick, light imprint of his lips sent a feathering of
sensual awakening over her entire body.

She backed hastily away. "Um, I've got lots of
work to do. Was there anything else you wanted to
tell me?"

"Just one thing." His gaze traveled over her,
from the smooth crown of her auburn head, down
the cream-colored linen suit that almost masked
her body's curves, down the graceful length of her
legs, to her dainty but flat-heeled shoes. "You look
beautiful this morning."

His compliment took her completely by surprise.
She knew she looked dignified and professionally
competent, because she'd worked very hard to project that image. But *beautiful?* It was true that
men had called her that before, but never when she
was dressed like this, armored for the business
world.

"Thank you," she said, and couldn't stop herself
from smiling at him. Darn it all, she was acting like
a cream puff! If she didn't watch out, Keith would
think she was a pushover for his flattery.

"Beautiful as a lion-taming goddess," he murmured. "With a heart full of warmth that glows in your eyes and sparkles in your laughter."

"Keith . . ." Her protest faltered. "Listen, I've got to go. See you tonight." She rushed to the door and had almost made it safely outside when his final words caught her like a silken net. All the rest of the day she would hear those words dance and echo in her head.

"Until tonight, goddess," he said.

Oh, dear. What on earth was she going to *do* about him? More importantly, what was she going to do about the impossible longings that crept into her own heart each time he spun his magic tales of predestined lovers and romantic meetings?

Char gave a sharp gasp and clutched at her bare chest. She backed swiftly away from the bathtub, never taking her eyes off the huge black spider that was lurking there with such sinister patience.

Oh, dear. She had never been fond of spiders. You might even say she was terrified of them. Regardless of the fact that her mother had seen fit to name her after one—the immortal heroine of *Charlotte's Web*.

"Mrs. Benson?" she called out in a quavering voice, grabbing her dark blue quilted robe off the hook on the door and shrugging it over her shivering shoulders. She opened the bathroom door and scurried out into the hall. "Mrs. Benson, there's a—"

"Can I help you?" The cold, scornful young voice right at her back caused Char to jump half a foot and whirl around. She faced two strangers—a young woman in her late teens and a girl with freckles and pigtails, who looked about twelve years old. The young woman's sullen eyes were half-hidden by a draping of short, side-parted straight brown hair, and the younger girl's mouth was twisted into a sneer. Or maybe it only looked that way because of the enormous wad of bubble gum she was chewing.

"You must be Ann and Lisa Benson," Char said, trying to regain her shaky composure. She managed a weak smile.

"Must we?" The young woman spoke tightly through fuchsia-colored lips. Beside her, the other girl's jaws revolved in a slow, steady, insolent rhythm.

"Aren't you?" Char asked uneasily. Suddenly *anything* seemed possible.

"So what if we are? What's it to you?" the pig-tailed imp piped up, folding her freckled arms across the front of her taxicab-yellow short-sleeved sweatshirt. Her lips puckered as a pink bubble began to grow out of her mouth.

"Hush, Lisa! Let me handle this!" Ann ordered in a loud whisper.

The bubble popped. "Why should I? I—"

"What seems to be the problem here?" A hostile male voice rumbled just over Char's left shoulder. This time she managed to restrain herself from giving a startled leap into the air. Slowly she turned her head. The owner of the voice was a slim, scowling young man with broad shoulders, sandy hair, and dark-rimmed glasses. Steve Benson, she presumed. The one who was studying to be a doctor.

Since the sisters were now stonily silent, Char decided it was up to her to answer him. "There's no problem," she said hastily. "I'm Charlotte Smith, your family's new boarder, and I was just introducing myself to your sisters."

The three Bensons looked at her as if she'd just

crawled out of a swamp. "But I thought I heard somebody screeching," Steve insisted.

Screeching? Had she really "screeched"?

"Um, yes, that was me," Char reluctantly admitted. She had a feeling the Bensons weren't going to be overly sympathetic about her fear of spiders. "You see, um, in the bathtub, I saw this—"

She stopped cold as her brain registered the swift, meaningful look that flickered between brother and sisters. Instantly suspicion dawned. Perhaps they already *knew* about the spider! And that would mean that they . . .

"You were saying . . . ?" Ann prompted.

"Gee, I forget," Char said sweetly, giving them her most cheek-pinching, saccharine smile. If they were going to play games with her, she could jolly well play games with *them*. "It's been a pleasure meeting you kids, but I have to go get dressed for my date tonight." Saying the words, she felt like a rookie bullfighter waving the red cape for the very first time.

Steve Benson's scowl deepened at her announcement, and the corded muscles in his arms clenched tighter. He eyed Char as if she were a scarlet woman polluting his home by her mere presence.

"You don't belong here," he said roughly. "Your coming here just makes trouble for everybody, and hurts someone who's already been hurt too much!"

"Steve!" Ann frowned a fierce warning at her brother. "Never mind him, Ms. Smith. I'm just dying to hear about your hot date." Her forced smile was edged with cunning. "Where's Mr. Webb taking you?"

"What makes you think my date is with Mr. Webb?" Char arched her brow over a cool blue stare, relishing the chance to give Ann a taste of her own medicine.

"Gosh, *isn't* it?" For the first time, the girl looked flustered. Her cheeks turned the same shade of pink as her sister's bubble gum.

Char was silent a moment, and then took pity on her. After all, the Bensons were only being loyal to their friend Debbie. Their hostile attitude was misguided but, under the circumstances, understandable.

"Yes, it is Keith Webb I'm having dinner with," she announced, noting with surprise how her pulse rate kicked up when she spoke his name. "Now you'll have to excuse me while I finish dressing."

She smiled, and retreated to the bathroom, hurrying to close the door and block out their staring faces. Only as she turned toward the tub did she remember . . . the spider.

It was gone.

Long minutes later, after searching every nook and cranny of the large room, Char reluctantly concluded that the spider had ventured down the bathtub drain. Oh, dear. "It looks like it's gotta be you or me, spider," she muttered squeamishly, inserting the drain plug and turning on the water. When she'd finished bathing and it was time to pull the plug and let her bath water go rushing down the drain, she winced. "Sorry, spider." Much as she disliked spiders, she didn't like destroying them either. It was a relief to get out of that bathroom and back to her own room.

Slipping out of her robe, Char picked up the silky, lace-trimmed underwear she'd laid out on the bed earlier, along with her dress for the evening. *Why* was she wearing her prettiest, flimsiest underthings for this date with Keith? Good question. Too bad she wasn't about to answer it.

A tiny sound from the direction of the nearest window made her turn around, and she frowned.

Because it was still light outside and the bedroom lay in shadow, with its window screened by the branches of a large tree, Char hadn't bothered to pull her shades down. Why should she? No one could see in. Not unless someone was sitting in the tree right outside her window. . . .

Even as she turned, the leaves rustled and she caught a flash of bright yellow amid the thick foliage. The same color yellow as Lisa's sweatshirt. How rude! Char flung her robe across her body like a shield and marched to the window.

"What the hell are you doing spying on me from that tree?"

No answer.

"I know you're there, Lisa."

Silence.

"What are you, some kind of pervert?"

The only response was a faint twitch of a branch, which might have been caused by the wind. Char gave up and yanked the shade down. "Spoiled brat!" she muttered as she tugged her underwear on. She reached for her dress.

The small green frog underneath the dress leaped for its freedom, rocketing upward as if shot from the mouth of a cannon. Char screamed. How could she help it, when the thing *sprang* at her like that?

From beyond the drawn window shade came the unmistakable sound of gleeful laughter.

Char seized the china vase of cut flowers off the mahogany nightstand. With one quick flick of her wrist, she removed the flowers. At the window, her hands moved fast as a hungry mosquito as she snapped the shade up and unhooked the screen. With all the strength and accuracy that had served her well on her high-school softball team, Char hurled the contents of the vase at the spot where she'd glimpsed that betraying flash of yellow.

A muffled shriek was followed by gasps and sputtering. The tree branches quaked as if a storm were approaching. But Char couldn't stay to enjoy her moment of triumph, because someone was knocking at her door.

Setting the empty vase back on the nightstand, she hurried to open the door. Her first thought on seeing Faye Benson there was that this slight woman with the tired, kind face was much too nice to be the mother of Steve, Ann, and Lisa! Her second thought was that she had just emptied one of Faye's vases over the head of one of Faye's daughters, and how was Faye going to feel about that?

"Hello, Faye. I suppose you're wondering—augh!" The little green frog hopped over Char's bare feet as it made its escape through the open door.

"Oh, Miss Smith, I'm so sorry!" Faye cried. "I've told Lisa a hundred times not to bring those things in the house! And how on earth did it get into *your* room?"

"It must have happened while I was taking my bath," Char said, poker-faced. She preferred to fight her own battles, and saw no reason to involve poor Faye in what was a private matter between her and Lisa. "But don't worry. There's been no harm done." Except for one slightly damp child, she mentally added.

Faye sighed. "I'm relieved that you're taking it so well, but I'll have to have a talk with Lisa. She needs to understand that not everyone is as crazy about frogs and lizards as she is."

Char thought Lisa understood that fact perfectly well already, but she kept her thoughts to herself.

Faye turned to go, and then stopped. "Mercy! I almost forgot what I came up here for." She beamed at Char. "Keith is waiting for you downstairs. Looking mighty handsome, I might add."

"Doesn't he always?" Char muttered disgustedly.

But she felt as if somebody had just lit a candle inside her. Or maybe *she* was the candle. Because her body was melting like hot wax at the thought of Keith—his voice, his smile, his touch.

She stepped out into the hall. "I'd better not keep him waiting," she said, and her voice sounded high and breathless.

Faye stared, and then giggled. "Don't you want to put some clothes on first?"

"Clothes?" Char glanced down, and gulped. Oh, dear. She was still in her slip.

The other woman shook her head. "You've sure got it bad, haven't you? But I can't say I blame you."

"You can't?" Char asked in a bewildered voice. Blame me for *what*? she wondered.

"Heck, no. What woman *wouldn't* fall in love with Keith Webb if he gave her half a chance?" She winked at Char. "You hurry up and get dressed, and I'll tell him you're almost ready."

Keith's grin was devilish as he escorted her down the steps of the Bensons' front porch. "Gorgeous as you look tonight, I can't say I wouldn't have preferred you the other way."

"*What* other way?" But she was afraid she knew.

"In just your underwear, of course."

"Dammit! Faye shouldn't have—"

"Shh. Temper, temper, Char. She just thought I'd be pleased to know—"

"I'll *bet* you were pleased!" Her skin crawled with embarrassment. It was bad enough that she should have acted like a moonstruck idiot, but to have Keith *know* about it was utterly galling. "Just don't let it go to your head!" she snapped.

"Too late. It already went to my head . . . like

wine! When Faye said . . ." His voice sank to a husky whisper, and he stopped in the middle of the sidewalk. His hands moved up to cup her shoulders as he looked hungrily into her face. "She said you were wearing nothing but a little bit of lace and lots of stars in your eyes."

I'll kill her, was Char's first thought, but she knew it wasn't really Faye she was angry with.

"That just goes to show," she said crisply, "that I'm a better actress than I thought. I've already managed to convince one person that I'm crazy about you."

Keith's face went still, but almost instantly his mouth turned down in the comical expression of a wounded clown. "You mean, it was all an act? Your little heart"—his right hand slid down to a spot over her left breast—"didn't go pitty-pat at the thought of seeing me again?"

Her "little heart" was thundering like a stampeding herd of wild horses beneath the warm pressure of his hand! And he knew it, too. Haughtily she plucked his hand off her chest. "Are you planning on feeding me tonight, or just standing around trying to cop a feel?"

"I'm open to suggestion." His outrageous grin was almost irresistible.

Almost, but not quite. Char fixed him with a frosty stare.

"In that case," he said hastily, "let's go eat."

It wasn't until they were in the Mercedes with their seat belts buckled and the key in the ignition that they discovered they couldn't go *anywhere*. Not by car, anyway.

"I don't get it," Keith said impatiently. "This car was running fine on the way over here!"

He got out and took a long, thorough look under the hood. Char got out, too, and watched his intent, frustrated expression. "What's wrong?" she asked hesitantly.

"Not a damn thing that I can see! So why won't it start?" He looked at her. "I don't suppose, in addition to being a beautiful, sexy, brilliant, and warm-hearted goddess, you also happen to be a whiz of an auto mechanic?"

She shook her head guiltily. "I always meant to take a class, but . . ."

"I was afraid of that. Oh, well. Nobody's perfect." He stared at the engine for a few seconds more, and then slammed the hood down. "Damn!"

"I guess we'll have to forget about our date now." She was amazed at how disappointed she felt.

"Not on your life!" He shot a suspicious look her way. "Hey, goddess, did you put a spell on my car so you could get out of having dinner with me?"

"Of course not! Don't be—" But then she caught the wicked glint in his eye.

"Just kidding. I know you really *want* to be with me, even though you're afraid to admit it."

"Ha!" Not one of her snappier comebacks, she admitted. It was hard to be snappy when he'd just hit the nail right on the head. She *did* want to be with him. "We can take my car," she suggested.

"I've got a better idea. Let's walk! It's going to be a beautiful night, with moonlight and roses and soft breezes. Why waste it cooped up inside a car?"

Why indeed? "All right," she said.

"Uh-oh. I forgot one small problem—dinner. We'd have to settle for someplace within walking distance." He gave her a worried look.

"What's so bad about that?"

"Our choices would be limited to pizza, burgers, or a hot beef sandwich with mashed potatoes. None of which is quite as romantic as the meal I'd been planning for our first date."

Char laughed and opted for the pizza, then went

inside to change her shoes. She wasn't about to walk clear across town in high heels, no matter how small the town happened to be. Luckily her sleeveless turquoise knit dress was simple enough for the more casual dining experience that now awaited them.

"Did you forget something, dear?" Faye asked, looking up from her pile of mending as Char walked by the living room. Ann and Lisa also glanced up from their card game, but Steve, who had his nose buried in the latest issue of *Popular Mechanics*, ignored her completely.

"No, but Keith's car won't start." For the second time that day, she was aware of an exchange of glances among the younger Bensons. She even detected a satisfied smirk that Lisa quickly hid behind her hand of cards. Suddenly she suspected that Keith's mysterious car troubles weren't so mysterious after all!

"What a shame!" Mrs. Benson exclaimed in genuine commiseration. "Steve, why don't *you* take a look at Mr. Webb's car?" She turned to Char with a proud, motherly smile. "My son is practically a genius when it comes to fixing cars."

"You don't say?" Char drawled. *I'll just bet he is*, she was thinking.

"Oh, Mom." Steve glared at his mother and turned red.

"Thanks for offering, but Keith and I have decided we'd rather walk tonight, anyway." Char gave them a dreamy smile. "Keith promises me there'll be moonlight and roses, so how could we pass up such a romantic outing?"

She almost laughed aloud at the three disgruntled faces that greeted her announcement. Only Faye was pleased. *Chalk up one for me*, Char thought.

But five minutes later, she mentally awarded

more points to the other side. That was because of the mouse that scurried out of her closet when she reached for a different pair of shoes.

There was no moonlight yet as she and Keith set off, but the sun flooded the air with pure gold evening light. Bright flower beds and emerald-green lawns glowed like jewels, while shade trees rustled and shimmered overhead.

Keith entwined his arm with hers. "There," he said in satisfaction. "Now we look like an old married couple out for an evening stroll."

"Hardly."

"Why not?"

"You look much too handsome and glamorous to be an old married man." And the pressure of his bare arm against hers was much too inflammatory.

"That's not true!"

Char just laughed at his indignant frown.

"I could be a *very* happily married man," he insisted. "As long as I had the right woman for my wife."

The warmth in his eyes made Char nervous. "But you still wouldn't look like an *old* married man," she quickly pointed out. "That's all I meant."

But she knew she'd meant more than that—she couldn't see Keith Webb as a likely candidate for settling down to just one woman and the tranquil joys of married life. Not with *his* incredible good looks and seductive, mercurial charm.

"I could wear a gray wig and carry a cane," he suggested. "Or I could even paint wrinkles on my forehead."

"It wouldn't do any good, Keith. You probably won't look *old* even when you're ninety."

"Dammit, Char, I'm not Peter Pan!" he growled.

"What are you so touchy about all of a sudden?"

He scowled. "Hell, I don't know. But I keep getting the feeling you're not taking me seriously. I *am* a responsible adult, you know."

"I'll remember that next time you're inventing some crazy tall tale about fate and goddesses and lions!"

"Dammit, there you go again! Just because I haven't abandoned my sense of all the magical possibilities in life—" His hand slid to her wrist and he spun her around so she was facing him. Quick as summer lightning, his hands closed over her shoulders, pulling her body close against his.

Electric heat seared her to the very core as his warm flesh made contact with hers all along the length of their bodies. And then his mouth was searching out the liquid fire that smoldered between her lips.

Char let herself go, surrendering to the irresistible, impossible explosion of desire he ignited in her. His hands moved on her back like the hands of an archer bending a bow, shaping her body into a taut, responsive curve that arched against the hard virility of his loins.

"Oh, Keith," she whispered thickly when his mouth released hers. Her hands crept to his neck to draw him close again, so that the dazzling sensual sweetness of their kiss could continue.

But he leaned his forehead against hers, and tried to catch his breath. He nuzzled her temple, and then kissed her eyelids. When he did nothing more except hold her tight against his pounding heart, she opened her eyes.

"Now, goddess. Tell me that's not magic," he said huskily.

Six

Char blinked. Magic? It was *insanity*. They were standing on a public sidewalk, for crying out loud! People were staring at them—she looked around and saw gray-haired ladies on porch swings, a man in a straw hat weeding a flower bed, two boys and a girl shooting baskets through a hoop over a driveway, and a baby in a stroller out for a walk with his parents. Didn't the folks in this town ever go inside and lock their doors and watch TV? she wondered.

But Keith hadn't even noticed their audience. His eyes were still intent on Char, and his pupils were dark and dilated with desire. "It *was* magic for you, too, wasn't it?" he asked urgently.

Char closed her eyes, unable to lie about something so important. "Yes." She sighed. "But that doesn't make it any less of a mistake."

"You're still sure about that?"

"*Yes.*"

"Then we'll just have to be careful to avoid any more mistakes tonight, won't we? Come on, goddess, let's go eat."

The pizza place was noisy. All the sound generated by a blaring jukebox, a row of beeping video games, and a crowd of junior-high-school kids bounced off the bare wooden tables and pine-paneled walls.

"Good Lord!" Keith said, gazing around him in awe. "Except for the video games, this place hasn't changed since the last time I brought a date here! Which was when I was fifteen years old, in case you're wondering," he quickly added.

Char laughed. "At least we don't have to worry about getting carried away by the romantic mood of our surroundings."

"Don't count on it. It's not where you are, it's whom you're with. And I could get carried away by *you* at any spot you care to name."

"How about Tahiti?" She hadn't meant to say it—good grief, she didn't want to *encourage* him!—but it popped out nonetheless. She was getting as bad as *he* was, coming up with silly fantasies at the drop of a hat.

"Yes, that could *definitely* be arranged."

Oh, dear. He sounded perfectly serious.

"Can we order our pizza now?" she asked hastily. Changing the subject to a debate over pepperoni, mushrooms, and anchovies seemed like a safe bet. Surely that would make him forget Tahiti.

But once they'd placed their order and retreated to a corner table, Keith raised his mug of beer to click against her glass of red wine. "To Tahiti," he said meaningfully.

"I was only kidding!"

"Well, *I'm* not. Tahiti sounds like a wonderful idea. Beaches, palm trees, sunsets, and balmy tropical nights. Just the two of us, naked under the stars . . ." He gave her an overdone, *melting* sort of glance that made her want to grit her teeth, slap his face, and jump on a plane for Tahiti. "When do we leave?" he asked.

"We are *not* going to Tahiti."

"How about Fiji, then?"

"*Keith*."

"Okay, okay. We'll drop the subject . . . for now. Let's talk about you, instead. Tell me about your childhood."

"Huh?"

"You know, back when you went to grade school and wore braces and—"

"How did you know I wore braces?"

"Just a lucky guess. You must have looked adorable."

The man was clearly out of his mind, Char thought.

"Do you have brothers and sisters, or were you an only child, like me?"

"I have two younger sisters." She purposely gave the bare minimum of information, hoping he'd stop probing.

"Go on," he said.

"With what?"

"Telling me about your childhood. Were you happy?"

A shadow crossed her face. "Um, *no*. Not very." Now what had possessed her to admit *that*? she wondered.

"Why not, goddess?" he asked gently, frowning at the look of sadness he saw in her eyes.

"Too many worries. My parents . . . didn't get along. You see, my father wasn't cut out to be a husband or a father. Or an adult, for that matter. He ran out on us when I was eight years old."

"Damn, that's tough, Char. I'm sorry."

"It *was* tough," she agreed. "But we survived. My mother had her librarian's degree, so she went back to work. Of course, in those days they didn't dream of paying a woman enough to support herself and three kids. I saw how she had to struggle and worry, and I worried right along with her."

"Knowing you, I bet you did a lot more than worry," Keith said. "You probably took on more than your share of responsibility, trying to help out."

"I looked after my sisters and helped with the housework. But I didn't mind *that*. It was the financial insecurity, the feelings of fear and helplessness about the future, that weighed me down. That, and hating my father for what he'd done."

"So you never had much chance at a childhood, did you, goddess?"

"There were good times too," she insisted. "Especially later, after Mom married my step dad. I love my family very much, Keith."

"That doesn't surprise me. You're a very loving person—I could feel that about you from the first."

"From the *first*, huh?" Though his words had moved her, she managed a mischievous grin. "Was that before or after you yelled at me, swore at me, accused me of lying about my name, and assumed I was part of a plot to expose your little white lie to Debbie?"

Keith groaned. "Just slightly after that," he confessed. "And you'll never let me live it down, will you?"

"Never."

Just then their pizza order was called, and Char was relieved when their conversation—what they managed of it between bites of pizza, that is—continued on a less personal level. Their talk of books, movies, music, and politics could have been the casual, getting-to-know-you patter of any couple out on a first date. Except . . .

Except *what*? she asked herself.

Except for the subtle but ever-present current of

strong sexual attraction between them. Except for the way she was beginning to recognize and savor every tone of Keith's voice, every expression of his face, and every gesture of his body. Except for the emotional intimacy they'd already shared. Except for the lingering memory of his kisses and caresses. Except for just about every darn thing imaginable, she concluded wryly.

Once they'd finished their meal and left the noisy pizza parlor for the cool, blossom-scented twilight of the summer evening, the sensual feelings between them seemed to intensify tenfold. This time, when Keith took her arm, his touch transmitted a thousand tingling messages of desire. And every message was answered by the secret response of her flesh.

"Come here," he whispered, putting his arm around her waist and pressing her slim length against his side.

"We can't walk like this," she said breathlessly.

"But we can *pretend* to walk. Like teenagers pretending to dance."

Char gave an unsteady laugh. "I've got news for you—unless we start moving forward, nobody's going to fall for this."

"Who cares?" He put out his tongue and licked the pale crescent shape of her ear, then let his lips wander down her neck.

"I care." But her words, hovering there in the dusk like the first pale stars in the evening sky, seemed to transform themselves and take on a meaning she'd never intended. They seemed to say that she cared for *him*. And oddly enough, now that the words had been spoken, she was dreadfully afraid they might be true.

There was a tiny but awkward pause. Char felt Keith's body go tense against her own and then, as if he'd consciously willed it, relax. "Right," he said crisply. "I almost forgot. You wanted us to keep a low profile, didn't you?"

"Yes." She was relieved he hadn't picked up on the unintended double meaning of her remark.

"Then I'd better get you home before we make front-page news."

She gave him a puzzled look.

"Before I make love to you right here on Main Street," he translated in a seductive growl.

"Oh!" She scuttled sideways like a startled crab.

Keith laughed and pulled her gently back into the warm curve of his arm. "Just kidding, goddess. When you and I make love, it's going to be something very private and very special."

When, not *if*, she noticed. *When* they made love. But she didn't bother to contradict him, because her voice would have wobbled out of control if she'd said one word.

They started walking again, arm in arm, up one street and down the next. Char felt too dazed by her own emotions to pay attention to where they were going. She just concentrated on the simple magic of sharing the rhythm of Keith's footsteps, feeling their bodies joined in forward motion as they wandered through the soft summer night.

"I'm curious." Keith's rich, deep baritone suddenly broke the intimate silence. "How did I get to be so lucky? How come a woman like you isn't already spoken for?"

"I might ask you the same—how come *you're* not 'spoken for'?" she countered quickly.

"Me?" His low laughter made her spine tingle. "I guess I just never met the right woman. Oh, I admit there was a time when I was so busy trying to get where I wanted to go that I probably wouldn't have recognized the 'right' woman if she'd hit me over the head with a magic wand. But then, once I started feeling ready for her to turn up in my life, she took her own sweet time about it!" he complained in an accusing tone.

"How thoughtless of her," Char said dryly.

"My sentiments exactly. But you still haven't answered my original question. Why is a goddess like you still footloose and fancy-free?"

She shrugged uneasily. "I don't know. My job, I guess. The few times I've gotten serious about anybody, it was always my job that seemed to come between us. Especially the traveling. We ended up not sharing enough, not being together enough to make it worthwhile."

"Your job must mean a lot to you, then?"

"Absolutely." She thought of how hard she'd worked to get where she was so she could feel in control of her life, financially secure and independent. She *needed* that feeling to keep at bay the old worries and fears she'd known as a child after her father's desertion.

"So you never thought of changing jobs, or taking advantage of your value to Brannon-Hale by requesting that they assign you a less grueling travel schedule?"

She shook her head fiercely. "Of course not! Boy, you make me mad! Just like a typical male, you're suggesting that *I* should have made all the compromises and sacrificed *my* career for the convenience of some man!"

"Dammit, that's not what I said at all!"

"It's not?" She stopped trying to tug her arm out of his and waited for his reply.

"*No*. I just meant . . . I'm surprised you've put up with the way Brannon-Hale keeps sending you all over the map, year after year, and at such cost to your personal life."

"It's my job," she said simply. But his words had awakened a flicker of doubt. Why *did* she put up with it? After five years with the company, wasn't it about time she started getting some of the more sought-after assignments, the ones that didn't demand so much travel?

But she didn't let Keith see her uncertainty. "Besides," she added ruefully, "my job hasn't had much effect on my personal life just lately. It seems that every time I meet a man who interests me, he turns out to be already taken. And I can hardly blame my job for *that*."

"*I'm* not taken." His voice, velvety soft in the darkness, made her pulse jump.

"Who said I was interested in *you*?" But she knew he could hear the smile in her voice.

"I could say a little bird told me. . . ." He ran his hand caressingly from her shoulder to her hip.

"Mmm?" She gave a shiver of pleasure at his touch.

"But that wouldn't be true." His breathing was fast and shallow, and he moved closer until his cheek was almost brushing hers.

"No?"

"Let's just say I read it somewhere." His lips lightly touched the crest of her cheekbone.

"You *read* it?" Her voice slipped up an octave, and she pulled an inch away from him.

"In your eyes, goddess," he whispered. "In your eyes." And then he was kissing her mouth with fierce, hungry concentration. Nobody had ever kissed her quite like that before, as if she were the ultimate life experience, meant to be tasted fully, urgently, savoringly, before she somehow slipped away.

But Char had no intention of slipping anywhere. There was no place she'd rather be than in Keith's arms, kissing him back with equal intensity.

"Gosh, Ms. Smith!" Ann Benson's brash young voice penetrated the sensual haze of their embrace. "My mother would ground me for two weeks if my boyfriend and I ever carried on like *that* in public."

Dazedly Char turned her head. Ann was leaning out the passenger window of a gargantuan, rust-corroded, low-slung automobile that obviously needed a new muffler.

"Yeah, *we* have to do it in private." The driver of the car chortled.

Ann frowned. "Will you hush up, Fred?"

The driver glowered at Ann. "Hey, I was just—"

A new voice joined the debate from the shadows of the car's backseat. "*Please*, you guys, let's just get out of here!" the voice tearfully implored, and Char felt the back of her neck prickle in recognition. It was Debbie. Oh, the poor kid, Char thought. It must be horrible to see the man you loved kissing another woman the way she and Keith had just been kissing. How embarrassing.

"You heard her, Fred!" a fourth voice growled, sounding an awful lot like Steve Benson. "*Step on it*, you jerk!"

Fred stepped on it, and the car pulled away with a loud roar of the engine and a prolonged squeal of the tires.

"*Well*." Char heaved a deep sigh.

"Yes, *well*. That sure broke the mood, didn't it?" Keith said wryly. "Do you suppose they were cruising around looking for us?"

"I'm certain of it! I wouldn't put anything past those Benson kids—you were so right about them! And that reminds me." She told him her suspicions regarding his car trouble that evening. "I'm positive they did it just to mess up our date."

"It would take more than car trouble to ruin a date with *you*. I've been having a wonderful time."

"So have I," Char admitted. After all, if she told him any different, he'd *know* she was lying.

They started walking back toward the Benson

place, but the mood had indeed been broken. Keith's hands were in his pockets now instead of draped at Char's waist. He seemed preoccupied with his own thoughts, not even noticing the moon climbing over the tops of the sycamore trees and raining silver light over everything.

"There's the moonlight you promised me," Char said. She could smell the roses, too, as their sweet, heady scent drifted past her on the breeze.

"Mmm," Keith said absentmindedly, and Char felt like giving him a swift kick. They were still two blocks away from the big yellow house on Maple Street when Keith suddenly exclaimed, "Hey! I think I just figured out how Steve Benson booby-trapped my car!"

"Oh, really?" She might have guessed. The man had been thinking about his car. Of course.

"Yeah, you know that scene in *Beverly Hills Cop* where the guy takes this fruit and stuffs it in the exhaust pipe of the car that's tailing him? Well—"

"I don't watch movies with violence and car chases," she said huffily.

"Well, *excuse* me." He grinned. "My point is, that's what Steve could have done to my car. I checked everything under the hood, but I never thought of looking at the tailpipe."

She shrugged. "I suppose it's possible. Anyway, you'll soon find out." She gestured up the street to where Keith's Mercedes was parked at the curb.

"Not necessarily. If there *was* a piece of fruit, it's probably been removed by now, to stop me from figuring out what happened."

Sure enough, the car's tailpipe looked completely innocent once they were close enough to inspect it. Not a trace of a banana, peach, orange, apple, plum, or pear.

"Oh, well," Keith said, taking Char's hand and heading through a gap in the hedge around the

Benson's yard. The lawn lay spread before them, silver in the moonlight, its borders etched with black where trees and tangled bushes cast dark shadows.

"But . . . aren't you going to see if your car will start now?" Char asked, forgetting she was mad at him. Now that her curiosity had been piqued, she wanted the mystery solved.

"In a hurry to get rid of me, goddess?" His breath softly stirred her hair as he stepped up close behind her, wrapping his arms around her waist and drawing her back against his muscled warmth.

"No, but—"

"Good." He kissed her ear and her throat, sending ripples of arousal down her spine. "Then let's stay right here and enjoy the moonlight. Unless . . ." A note of deviltry crept into his voice. "Unless you were hoping we could get in my car and drive to my place for the night." His hands moved up her rib cage to brush the undersides of her breasts through the turquoise knit of her dress.

Char forced herself to disregard the long tremor of temptation his touch evoked. "Are you kidding? Faye would be scandalized. She'd probably ground me for a month!"

"Is that a yes or a no?" he whispered as his hands moved still higher, cupping the fullness of her breasts.

"Keith." She sighed. "You know it's a no."

"I was afraid of that." His sigh echoed hers as his hands dropped to her hips, molding her soft curves against the urgent pressure of his loins. "I want you so badly, Char."

"I know." She wanted him too. She ached with wanting him. "But isn't this the mistake we promised ourselves we wouldn't make?"

"It doesn't feel like a mistake, goddess." He turned her in his arms and brought his lips to hers, sparking the same sweet magic that had pulsed between them from the very first kiss. Once again the shared bewitchment cast a treacherous spell of forgetfulness, and Char sank to the grass in Keith's arms.

In that timeless instant, it no longer seemed to matter that their business relationship made it unwise and unprofessional for them to do what they were doing. And all Char's doubts and suspicions about Keith's whimsical character seemed to fade like morning mist. There was only the urgent, shuddering pleasure of his hands and lips caressing her as they lay entwined in the shadows.

His hard, warm body covered hers, and his hand brushed aside her skirt and glided up the silken length of her thigh. She gave a low moan as his palm pressed intimately against her, while his lips traveled first the outline of her breasts and then the hard ridge of her nipples through her dress.

She gripped his shoulders, acutely aware of the furnacelike heat of his smooth, muscled flesh beneath the white cotton shirt he wore. Her own skin was flushed and burning with desire, and she welcomed the feel of the cool night air against her back as Keith eased open the zipper of her dress.

And then, without warning, the night exploded with the hiss and shock and cold, wet impact of half a dozen sprinklers turned on full blast.

Char shrieked and tore herself out of Keith's arms. She stumbled across the lawn, half-blinded by the silvery-white needles of spray erupting everywhere around her. By the time she reached the back steps of the house, she was soaked to the skin. Her hands shook as she struggled with the zipper of her dress. Her brain didn't seem to be functioning too well, either.

"This can't be happening," she said, groaning through chattering teeth just as the porch light above her went on. Faye Benson peered out the screen door, wearing a cotton print bathrobe and an anxious frown.

"Oh, Miss Smith! What's happened to you? I heard a scream—"

A warm, strong arm closed tightly around Char's waist, supporting her trembling frame. "We got caught in the sprinklers, Faye," Keith said in a reassuring, matter-of-fact voice, while his fingers neatly and unobtrusively slid Char's zipper into place.

"The sprinklers? But . . . oh, mercy!" Faye gazed in astonishment at the gushing, whooshing frenzy taking place on her lawn. "They're not supposed to be on now," she said with a bewildered shake of her head. And then her gaze returned to the dripping, bedraggled couple at the foot of the steps. "You poor things!" she exclaimed. "Come inside and get dry!"

By the time they reached the door, she had an armload of towels ready to greet them. "You go on up and change, dear," she advised Char. "And you step in there, Keith, and get out of those wet clothes. I'll send Lisa to borrow something of Steve's for you to wear. Lisa!" she called.

"Yeah, Mom?" The diminutive figure seemed to materialize instantly from the shadows of the kitchen.

"Mercy! You startled me, Lisa! What on earth were you doing down here in the dark?" Faye gave the girl a sharp, suspicious look. "You wouldn't happen to know anything about the sprinklers going on just now, would you?"

Char, already halfway out the kitchen door on her way to change, froze and held her breath. Of course Lisa would deny everything, she thought.

"Sure. *I* turned them on," Lisa said flatly.

"Whatever for? We've had plenty of rain lately, and now just look what you've done to Mr. Webb and Ms. Smith—they're soaked! Shame on you, Lisa."

"Sorry." But Char knew Lisa wasn't one bit sorry, especially when the girl said slyly, "I only turned the water on because I heard two cats going at it on the lawn, and I wanted to break it up."

That little creep! Char's fists clenched in rage and humiliation. *Two cats indeed!* And how much had that precocious twelve-year-old actually *seen?* she wondered with a guilty pang. Oh, dear. She and Keith must have been out of their minds to carry on like that.

Keith's voice held an unmistakable quiver of amusement. "*I* didn't hear any cats—did you, Char?" He was taking the whole thing pretty darn lightly, she thought.

"No, but I did notice a little female *dog* around here," Char said nastily.

Lisa gave an appreciative snort. "You mean a little bitch, don't you, Ms. Smith?"

"*Lisa!*" her mother exclaimed in horror. "That's *not* a nice word to use. Now, march upstairs and bring me your brother's robe. And then go straight to your room! You and I are going to have a serious talk."

"But, Mom—"

"You heard me, young lady!"

Sending a baleful glance in Char's direction, Lisa stomped out of the kitchen. Faye looked ready to rush into anxious apologies, but Char forestalled her.

"Oh dear, I'm dripping all over your floor!" she said, and beat a hasty retreat.

* * *

When she came downstairs ten minutes later, she was wearing jeans and a mint-green cotton sweater, and her wet hair was draped over a towel around her shoulders.

Keith and Faye were sitting at the kitchen table, sipping mugs of hot cocoa. Keith's dark hair gleamed damply in the warm yellow light, and the lapels of his borrowed robe didn't quite meet across his chest, revealing a broad expanse of tanned muscle and dark chest hair. He looked sexy as hell.

Char noticed he had that teasing sparkle in his green eyes, but for once it wasn't directed at her. Faye was still laughing and blushing like a teenager over whatever he'd said before Char walked in. A sudden chill, which had nothing to do with her wet hair, inched up Char's spine. Damn him and his easy, effortless charm, she thought.

Faye handed her a mug of cocoa, and Keith gave her a look that seemed to caress her flushed face and glowing mane of damp auburn hair. "You've got to watch this man of yours!" Faye said, smiling. "He says such wicked things."

"I've noticed." She took a gulp of cocoa that scalded her tongue.

"Now, Faye!" Keith protested. "I was only saying what everybody knows—that Bill Foster had a mighty big smile on his face when he showed up at work the morning after his date with you last week. He didn't *say* anything, mind you . . . but he sure did smile."

"I guess he liked getting some home cooking for a change," Faye said with a twinkle in her eye.

"That must be it," Keith solemnly agreed, and Char felt the tension inside her ease a bit. He hadn't been flirting with Faye—just charming her socks off by teasing her about Bill Foster. Still, she felt uneasy at the way he always knew exactly the right thing to say to make a woman happy. How could she trust a man like that? How could she be sure he *meant* the things he said?

There was a noise at the front door, and then Ann and Steve tramped down the hall into the kitchen. They didn't look too happy to see Keith and Char there. Steve's perpetual scowl deepened when he saw that Keith was wearing *his* bathrobe, and that it was too small for the older man's broad shoulders and chest.

Faye jumped up to fix more hot cocoa. "We had to borrow your robe for Mr. Webb while his clothes are in the dryer," she said to Steve. "Your sister accidentally turned the sprinklers on him and Ms. Smith. Did you kids enjoy the movie?"

The expression on Ann's face switched from barely controlled laughter at news of the sprinkler incident, to uneasiness at her mother's last question. "Um, actually, Mom, we got there late, so we decided to just drive around instead."

Faye sighed and looked worried. "Fred must have liked that. I do hope you behaved yourselves. And drove carefully."

"Oh, Mom," Ann said impatiently. "Of course we did."

There was an awkward pause. "Speaking of driving," Keith said, "I may not be able to drive home tonight, with the car trouble I'm having."

"You're welcome to stay here," Faye offered. "We've got a couple of extra beds."

"Just one bed should do me fine," he said smoothly, with a sly wink at Char that made her turn pink. Oh, dear. Keith *here*, under the same roof? He was perfectly capable of sneaking to her room in the middle of the night, she knew. But was she capable of sending him away if he did?

Steve Benson was in the process of choking on his hot cocoa. "You should try starting your car again," he suggested as he wheezed. "Maybe it just needed a chance to cool down." His voice sounded desperate.

"Could be. But the offer of a bed is *very* tempting." Keith grinned so wickedly that Ann looked back and forth from him to Char in shocked amazement. Ann had never seen a middle-aged person—someone over thirty—give anyone a look like *that* before. For the first time she had an inkling of what her best friend, Debbie, must have seen in the handsome but rather boring and certainly *old* Mr. Keith Webb to make her go bonkers over him.

Faye Benson also noticed Keith's naughty grin, and she had to smother a smile as she said, very firmly, "On second thought, if your car doesn't start, Steve had better drive you home. I'm sure that old car he's been working on all summer must be fixed up enough by now for a trip out to your place. Right, Steve?"

Steve's face was a study in frustration. Clearly he wanted to say yes. But just as clearly he knew the car wouldn't even make it around the block.

Char spoke up quickly. "Steve is welcome to use *my* car to take Keith home."

Keith gave her a reproachful look. "I wouldn't dream of putting Steve to so much trouble," he said.

"It's no trouble," Steve growled.

"I'll check to see if your clothes are dry," Char swiftly volunteered, bolting out of her chair. In the laundry room, she found that Keith's clothes were still a trifle damp, but that didn't stop her from ruthlessly pulling them out of the dryer.

Turning with the pile of clothing in her arms, she found herself face-to-face with Keith. His large frame blocked the door of the laundry room.

"In a hurry to get rid of me?" He softly repeated

the question he'd asked earlier in the shadows on the moonlit lawn.

It took a lot of willpower, but this time her response was different. "*Yes.* I'm tired, and I have to get up early for work tomorrow."

Keith eyed the stern line of her jaw, and sighed. "Then I'd better go. What time shall I pick you up for dinner tomorrow night?"

"Never. Once is enough. I'm not going out with you again until my command performance at the dinner dance on Saturday."

"But Char, what about the Bensons? We've got to convince them that—"

"That story won't work anymore, Webb. The Bensons have seen enough tonight to last the rest of the week. If they haven't figured out by now that we can't keep our hands off each other, they must be blind!"

"You may have a point there. But it couldn't hurt to—"

"No. Good night, Keith." Char held out the stack of clothes, and he reached out to take it. But then his hand bypassed the clothes and circled her wrist instead, tugging her gently into his arms.

His kiss made her tremble. She closed her eyes, letting the sweet persuasion of his mouth almost convince her that she was cruel and heartless to send him away. His chest was warm and bare and softly hairy under her touch as she lifted her hand toward his shoulders. He pulled her more tightly against him, and she felt the scant coverage of his robe give way to his hard, bare thighs.

"Are you two at it *again*?" Ann asked, standing on tiptoe to try to peer over Keith's shoulder into the laundry room.

Keith loosened his hold on Char and quickly readjusted the ebbing folds of the robe. "We were just saying . . . good night," he said thickly.

"Right. Good night," Char muttered breathlessly as she bent down to pick up the clothes she'd dropped in the heat of the embrace. Keith practically grabbed the wad of clothing out of her hands, and instantly positioned it at a strategic spot over his upper thighs.

"Gosh, Ms. Smith, what's so funny?" Ann asked when Char couldn't hold back her laughter at Keith's attempt to be nonchalant.

"N-nothing," she sputtered.

"Don't mind her," Keith said to Ann. "She always gets hysterical when I kiss her."

Char snorted in protest, and went off into a fresh burst of laughter.

Ann rolled her eyes. "Whatever turns you on."

"It does," Keith said. "Believe me, it does."

Ten minutes later, Char waved good night from the Bensons' front porch as Keith, wearing damp, rumpled clothing, started his car and drove away.

Seven

Char closed the door of the phone booth, readied her long-distance calling card, and took a deep breath. At the sight of the rather ancient telephone, she felt a twinge of uneasiness. Even a little town like Webb Falls must have a fully automated phone system in this day and age . . . mustn't it? There couldn't possibly be one of those legendary switchboard operators who listened in on everybody's calls and knew the whole town's business . . . could there?

She decided to play it safe. There was no need to explain the whole loony situation to her sister over the phone. All she really wanted right now, at ten A.M. on the Saturday of the Webb Falls annual dinner dance, was a strong dose of her baby sister's ebulliently upbeat personality.

"Hi—omigosh—hold on—I'll be right back!" a breathless, husky voice exclaimed on the fifth ring. That was Pippi, all right. Pippi, like Charlotte and their sister Arrietty, had been named after a character in a children's storybook—in Pippi's case, the irrepressible redhead Pippi Longstocking. And there were times when she was as madcap and wacky as her namesake.

Char tapped her foot impatiently as the minutes passed and the long-distance charges between Minneapolis and upstate New York kept adding up. She had hoped that Pippi's marriage to a steady, sensible accountant, who also happened to be the sweetest, most lovable man in Minneapolis, might make her a tad less impulsive, but no such luck. Jeremy adored Pippi just the way she was, and wasn't about to try to change her.

"Hi—I'm back—who is it?"

"It's me. Or 'It is I,' as Mom would say."

"Char! Sorry I kept you waiting so long, but I was throwing up."

"You were *what*?" She couldn't believe her ears. Pippi was never sick.

"Throwing up. Isn't it exciting?"

"It *is*?" Oh, dear. Pippi had really flipped her lid this time.

"Char . . . I've got morning sickness!"

"You mean, you're *pregnant*?" Char felt as if she'd just had the wind knocked out of her. Her baby sister was going to be a *mother*!

"I should hope so! Otherwise I've made a liar out of my doctor. And I'll have been losing my Cheerios every morning for no good reason."

"Pippi, what wonderful news! Congratulations! Do Mom and Dad and Arri know?"

"I'm calling them later this morning."

"And how's Jeremy taking it?"

"Just like an accountant. Would you believe he's already planning an investment portfolio for the kid's college education? That is, when he's not fussing over me like a mother hen, or talking baby talk to my tummy."

"He'll make a wonderful father," Char said,

unable to keep a wistful note out of her voice. "You can always count on Jeremy."

"I know," Pippi said lovingly.

"He's so solid and dependable. Not like—"

"Our own father?" Pippi suggested wryly.

"Definitely not like *him*. But I was actually thinking of someone else—a man I know here in Webb Falls. This guy is so sexy and handsome you could die, and the way he talks, he could charm the birds out of the trees, but . . ."

"But?"

"Oh, Pippi, I'm so worried and confused. Even though I know he's all wrong for me, I think I'm falling for him in a big way."

"*How* is he wrong for you? Isn't he interested in you?"

"Yes, he is, but—"

"Is this guy single, I hope?"

"Yes, but—"

"Hooray! At least he's not another of your silly crushes on men who aren't available. So what's wrong with him, Char?"

"For your information, I am twenty-nine years old and I do *not* indulge in 'silly crushes,' " she said icily.

"Oh, sure. What else would you call it when the only men you've let yourself feel any interest in are the ones you know you can't have? I wonder sometimes if you aren't afraid of a real commitment."

"That's a horribly unfair thing to say! You know the way my job keeps me shuttling from one city to the next—"

"Are you sure that isn't just another excuse?"

"Pippi! What's gotten into you?" Char felt on the verge of tears. Why was her youngest sister suddenly picking on her like this?

"I'm just worried about you, Char! I want you to

be happy, the way Jeremy and I are happy. But if you keep on the way you're going . . ."

"Save the lectures, all right?" Somehow she kept her voice steady. "Listen, I'm thrilled about the baby, and I'll call again in a couple of weeks. 'Bye."

"Char, wait—"

But Char quietly put the receiver back on the hook, and bit her lip as she stared out the clear sides of the phone booth. Twenty feet away, the gas pumps of the filling station were red blurs behind the tears in her eyes.

Darn Pippi anyway, Char thought. Didn't her sister know that men as wonderful as Jeremy didn't grow on trees? And Pippi was a fine one to talk—her love life had been one disaster after another until she'd finally fallen for the mild-mannered accountant who, she'd once claimed, wasn't even her type.

But . . . oh, horrors . . . could Pippi possibly be right? *Am I afraid of a real commitment?* Char asked herself. Here she was almost thirty years old, and both her younger sisters were more emotionally settled than she was—Pippi with Jeremy and now a baby on the way, and Arri with her dull but dependable fiancé, John.

Char's thoughts, as always, returned to Keith. It was true that she was afraid of her feelings for him. Who *wouldn't* be afraid, when the man's touch could evaporate all her good intentions and tempt her to do what she knew wasn't right?

But her fears went beyond that. When you loved someone, you had to depend on him, one way or another. And she'd never wanted to depend on anyone, ever again. Not after the first man in her life—her father—had let them all down so cruelly. Maybe a part of her *had* shied away from commitment, for that very reason. But if so, she hadn't been fair, because not all men were like her father. Now the question was, was Keith?

"You just missed the delivery van," Faye announced when Char returned from making her unsatisfying phone call to Pippi and running several errands.

"Oh, dear. Doesn't he know when to stop?" She sighed. "What did he send *this* time?"

"Just your flowers for the dance tonight."

"That's all? No more exotic fruit baskets or extravagant floral arrangements?"

Faye shook her head reprovingly, clearly indicating to Char that she ought to show a little more appreciation for the romantic offerings Keith had showered on her since their date four days ago.

"Thank goodness!" His first gift had overwhelmed her . . . and touched her. How could she resist six dozen long-stemmed roses and a card that read, "Remember the moonlight, the roses, and me"? As if she would ever forget!

But on Thursday the delivery man had staggered under a gigantic floral display of exotic tropical blossoms—hibiscus, bougainvillea, orchids, and other flower species Char couldn't even begin to name. "Think Tahiti," the card read. Again she'd felt overwhelmed, but also a little uneasy. There was something too lordly and lavish in the gesture. It was the kind of gift an eighteenth-century rake might send his latest mistress.

On Friday the "Tahiti" theme had recurred with a gigantic basket of tropical fruit. She had to give Keith credit for originality and dramatic innuendo when it came to the attached card: "If you're hungry for forbidden fruits . . . think of me." Reading that, she'd trembled. But then annoyance had taken over. He was exposing her to gossip by sending such ostentatious gifts. And if he thought that kind of flashy bid for attention was going to have her swooning at his feet, he was dead wrong!

Now, as she gazed down at the beautiful, delicate blooms he'd sent for her to wear that night, and as she remembered the painful things her sister had said to her that morning, she felt confused. She wanted so much to be with Keith, but she had so many doubts. And her sister couldn't explain them all away by telling her she was afraid of commitment. What she was afraid of was giving her heart to someone who would carelessly break it—someone as charming and irresponsible as her father had been.

But was Keith really like that? Maybe he was sincere when he said all those wonderful things that sounded too good to be true. Lord, she hoped so! But until she knew for sure, she had to be careful. She mustn't jump into bed with him, no matter how fierce the yearning or intense the fire. After all, she hadn't known him very long . . . and he was still her client. They had to try to be more discreet about the relationship they were *pretending* to have, because she didn't want people thinking she *would* sleep with a client. But . . . someday he wouldn't be a client anymore. The artificial barriers between them would be gone. What would happen then?

"Did you miss me, goddess?" Their bodies touched lightly as Keith walked her to his car. He looked absolutely stunning in a white dinner jacket and black trousers, and Char's bare-shouldered dress of dark peacock blue shimmered in the light from the streetlamp. Keith's gift of orchids and sweet-smelling freesias gleamed palely in her hair.

"Why would I miss you? I've seen you every day at work. And I've had more than enough flowers and fruit to remember you by," she said pointedly.

"Uh-oh. Did I overdo it? I find it damn near impossible to be restrained and rational where you're concerned."

Damn. How did he always manage to say the one thing that was guaranteed to melt her like butter? But she wasn't about to let him know it.

"Yes, you did overdo it a little." He looked so crushed at her words that she added huskily, "I loved the roses, though."

His face lit up like a sunrise. "I'm glad. And I want you to know how much I missed you. Seeing you at work just wasn't the same."

It hadn't been the same for her either. She had missed him too. But she wasn't ready to confess just how much. *Be careful*, she reminded herself as they approached his parked car.

"Ah-ha. Here's another piece of fruit to add to your collection," Keith announced, stooping to remove a peach from the exhaust pipe of the Mercedes. "Someone wants to keep Cinderella from attending the ball."

Because of Debbie, Char thought, dreading the awkward meeting that was bound to take place between the young woman and herself that night.

"I'm not surprised," she said aloud. "They've been trying all week to drive me out of town."

"Oh?" He frowned.

"Just little things. Frogs, worms, snakes, you name it."

"Why didn't you tell me? I'll—"

"Keith. Let me handle it myself. I'm tougher than I look."

"But you wouldn't be having these problems at all if I hadn't—"

"Shh. The bushes have ears around here. Let's

go to the dance." She smiled up at him, and he caught his breath.

"Yes. Let's. But first . . ." He gathered her into his arms and met her lips in a kiss that was like plunging over the top of a waterfall. It felt so achingly right to be in his arms again. They were both trembling and breathless by the time they broke apart and got in the car to head for the dance.

It was a mob scene. As Keith and Char, arm in arm, threaded their way through the crowd, Char stared around her in awe. Surely everybody in town was there, dressed to kill. And, as she suddenly noticed, they were all staring right back at her and Keith, probably sizing her up to see whether she was a suitable companion for Webb Falls's most eligible bachelor. Were they comparing her to Debbie? she wondered uneasily. But why should she care if they were? What she really ought to worry about was how she could possibly keep a low profile after *this*!

In an effort to ignore the curious looks, Char concentrated on the scene around her. Webb Falls Municipal Park had been transformed for the occasion with colored lanterns, a large temporary dance floor, barbecue pits, kitchen tents, and row upon row of tables draped with white cloth. "What do they do if it rains?" she asked Keith over the sound of the musicians tuning up in the nearby band shell.

"Are you kidding? No drop of rain would dare to show itself at any social event organized by my Aunt Agnes and her cronies!"

"That's a handy talent."

"Yes, she's got even the weather browbeaten into cooperation. You see now why—"

He stopped walking so suddenly that Char, whose arm was still linked with his, almost lost her balance.

"Speak of the devil," he muttered. "Quick, this way—maybe she hasn't spotted me yet."

Before Char could figure out what he was talking about, he swerved around a small knot of people and ducked behind a hydrangea bush, dragging her after him.

"Keith Wilbur Webb!" a loud, matronly voice scolded from behind them. "Come back here this minute and introduce me to your friend!"

"*What* did she call you?" Char asked, startled.

"Just my name."

"Your middle name is *Wilbur*?"

He nodded. "Dumb name, **right**? That's why I use just the initial." He peered over the hydrangeas. "Uh-oh, she's heading this way."

Wilbur, Char thought. Oh, dear. Oh, help! Maybe fate *was* bringing them together, as a practical joke! Luckily, Keith seemed never to have read *Charlotte's Web*. He didn't know about Charlotte the spider and Wilbur the pig.

"I know you're there, young man!" The woman's steely voice boomed from the other side of the bush.

Keith sighed and stood up, flashing a sheepish grin. "Hello, Aunt Agnes. How nice to see you." He patted Char's hand and led her out to meet a tiny, white-haired lady in lavender, who looked fragile as a porcelain figurine.

"Well, what have you got to say for yourself?" Aunt Agnes demanded after Keith had swept her up in an enthusiastic bear hug and made the introductions. "Why is your poor old auntie the last person in town to meet this stunning young woman?"

"I didn't want to bother you, since I knew how

busy you'd be organizing all this." He gestured to the hustle and bustle taking place all around them.

"Nonsense. I could manage this in my sleep, and you know it. The truth is, you were afraid of what I might say about Debbie."

Keith swallowed. "Aunt Agnes—"

"Don't bother to deny it! You silly boy, how could you think I would try to interfere with your decision in a matter like this?"

"Well, um—"

"Just because your choice of a bride is so terribly important to the whole family and to the entire community is no reason why you should listen to *me*! Just because Debbie Forrest is a lovely, well-bred young girl from an excellent family, and just because she adores the ground you walk on, is no reason—"

"*Thank you*, Aunt Agnes! I'm so glad we agree. What a load off my mind! Well, Char and I had better start mingling—people will feel insulted if we monopolize your delightful company much longer. Give my love to Uncle Eliot."

"But—"

"So long, Aunt Agnes." He whisked Char away so fast she was out of breath by the time they stopped. "Whew! Bet you didn't know I was such a fast talker, did you, Char?"

She felt a funny little jab inside when he said that, though maybe it was only a stitch from all the running. "You lose your bet. I've always known you were a fast talker. What I didn't realize was that you were such a fast *runner*." She rubbed her arm to see if the circulation was coming back yet.

"With Aunt Agnes, you have to be both. I didn't want to land you in a family quarrel in front of the whole town, so I had to cut her off and get away before she started implying unforgivable things about you."

"Was she really going to do that?"

"Oh, yes. You don't know Aunt Agnes. Her next sentence would have been something like, 'Just because Ms. Smith is a career woman whose family we never heard of and just because we know nothing about her past, which may be full of faceless men, drugs, and poor dental hygiene, is no reason you shouldn't ruin your life and break your poor old auntie's heart by marrying her.' "

"Oh, dear. My word. Are you serious?" Char couldn't help laughing at his perfect mimicry of his aunt.

"I'm serious. But don't worry. I love her because she's my aunt, but I *never* take her advice."

"Why should I worry? We both know there's no question of your *marrying* me, for heaven's sake!"

Keith didn't say anything.

"Oh, look, there's Faye," Char said quickly. "Is that man with her the Bill Foster you were teasing her about?"

"That's Bill. They look pretty happy together, don't you think?"

"Very happy." They went over and spent a few minutes chatting with the older couple, and then it was time to find their seats for dinner. People were still eyeing them curiously as they made their way through the line at the lavish buffet and then returned to their table with loaded plates.

"You'd think I was wearing a sign that said 'ogle me,' " Char muttered.

"Relax. They're probably all like me—they can't take their eyes off you because you're so damn sexy in that dress."

"*Is* it the dress?" Char asked anxiously. "Did I wear the wrong thing?"

"Of course not. You look wonderful." Keith gripped her hand reassuringly. She darted a nervous glance around the crowd and saw that her dress was, indeed, perfectly in keeping with what the other women her age were wearing. So why was everybody *watching* her like this? Were they waiting to see what would happen when she came face-to-face with Debbie?

At their table she found it hard to make polite dinner conversation with people who insisted on staring at her as if she had three heads. If only she and Keith could slip away by themselves, she thought longingly. Just for some peace and quiet. Then she had to laugh. Whom was she trying to kid? Being alone with Keith wouldn't be peaceful at all. It would be breathlessly exciting. Insane and unwise. In a word, wonderful.

She could tell that Keith was having similar thoughts. There was no mistaking the way his eyes went dark when he looked at her and the way his thigh brushed seductively against hers under the table.

"Don't be crazy!" she whispered when his hand caressed her knee and started inching higher. "I told you, I'm no actress. If you keep that up, everybody at this table will guess what's going on, just by the look on my face."

"Let them guess, goddess. Will it be a smile?"

"What?"

"Will the look on your face be a smile?"

"What an ego! *No*," she lied. "It'll be a look of total embarrassment."

"Then I'd better stop." His hand retreated, and Char couldn't deny that she felt a teensy bit disappointed. What was happening to her, to her carefully preserved professional image? One week ago no one could have convinced her she'd even be *tempted* to play hanky-panky under the table with a client. Especially not with an entire town looking on! She gnawed delicately on a piece of barbecued chicken as the worried thoughts rushed through her head.

"Do you have any idea how sexy you look trying to lick that barbecue sauce off your mouth?" Keith's voice held a husky warmth that went beyond teasing.

Instantly she pulled in her tongue and reached for her napkin.

"No, let me," he said, taking the napkin from her trembling fingers. Char felt her face tingle and grow warm as with slow, careful strokes he wiped away the last traces of barbecue sauce. Conversation at the table hushed as the other diners looked on with interest. People at other tables were watching too. "There, you're all perfect again," Keith said.

"I never claimed to be perfect. And you're crazy if you think I am."

Keith just smiled.

Volunteers poured coffee at each table. Dinner was almost over, and all Char could think of was that in just a few minutes the dancing would begin and she would feel Keith's arms around her again. She would nestle against his chest and hear the accelerating thud of his heartbeat. Anticipation surged inside her until she was almost dizzy with it.

When Aunt Agnes stood up at a nearby table and introduced—at length—the first after-dinner speaker, Char almost groaned aloud. They couldn't do this to her! Her impatience to dance with Keith was like a fever in her blood, a hunger. The very molecules of her body seemed to cry out for contact with him.

As she listened impatiently, she learned that the dinner dance this year was a fund-raiser for the community hospital. When the mayor got up to speak, Char felt a faint spark of interest, simply because he was Debbie's father. But with his opening words, he had her complete attention.

"As most of you know, it was just about a year ago that my daughter was severely injured in a head-on collision with a drunk driver who swerved into her lane. I firmly believe that, were it not for our outstanding community hospital and its well-equipped, expertly staffed emergency room, my daughter would not be alive today."

Char saw, in the faces around her, that others were as moved by his words as she was.

"We're lucky, in a town this size, to have the fine hospital we do. But it took more than luck to get it. It took hard work, individual generosity, and community support. All of you here tonight are continuing that support, and I thank you, as a parent, from the bottom of my heart. But there is one man who deserves our special thanks for his unstinting generosity and commitment on behalf of our hospital. I give you . . . Keith W. Webb!"

The crowd erupted into enthusiastic applause. Char turned to Keith in pleased surprise, and found him ducking his head and blushing. "Sorry about this, goddess," he mumbled as he pushed back his chair and stood up. "I had no idea he would make such a big deal out of it."

Watching Keith walk to the microphone, Char felt her chest bursting with pride and another emotion she wasn't ready to name. She was seeing a side of Keith she hadn't even guessed at. Of course she had known, after a week at the Webb Company, how much he was respected and admired by his employees, and that should have told her something. But she had persisted in seeing him as an untrustworthy spellbinder, spinning magic tales and beguiling her with his irresistible good looks and bold sensuality.

Now, for the first time, she realized how seriously he took his community responsibilities. He was a man committed to making the world a better place. And it was time for her to reexamine her own attitude toward him. After all, if an entire town felt it could depend on him, why couldn't she?

"Thank you," Keith said into the microphone. "First let me say, I don't deserve any special thanks. The way I look at it, we're all just doing our share for Webb Falls." He grinned. "But I do have a reason to be up here talking to you tonight. On behalf of the fund-raising committee, I'm pleased to announce that we've established a scholarship to encourage promising young people from Webb Falls to pursue careers in medicine. And we've already selected the first recipient. Will Steve Benson please come up here?"

Char clapped and cheered with the rest of the crowd, and reached for the nearest napkin to wipe away the happy tears welling in her eyes. She was so pleased for Faye, for Steve, for the whole family. This scholarship would mean so much to them. And she had a hunch that Keith had had a lot more to do with it than he was letting on.

"You were wonderful!" she whispered huskily when the brief ceremony was over and Keith had returned to his seat. She wanted to hug him, but not with so many people watching.

"Don't *you* start that stuff," he said gruffly. "I'm counting on you to keep me from getting an inflated ego. You're the one who's supposed to spit in my eye and tell me I'm full of beans."

"Okay, you're full of beans." She smiled saucily. "But I still say you were wonderful."

He grinned. "If you insist, goddess. And now that we've established what a marvelous fellow I am, how about dancing with me?"

"I thought you'd never ask."

Her heart was racing with excitement as they

approached the dance floor. All evening she had wanted to be in Keith's arms, and now the moment was here at last. His eyes locked with hers as his open palm slid along the curve of her spine.

"Gosh, Ms. Smith! Mr. Webb!" a familiar voice exclaimed behind them. "How'd you two *get* here, anyway?"

Sighing in unison, Char and Keith turned to face Ann Benson and her boyfriend, Fred. "We drove in Keith's car, of course," Char said, smiling as serenely as she could.

"Oh." Ann frowned. "You didn't have any . . . car trouble, or anything?"

"Heavens, no! Why do you ask?" She noticed out of the corner of her eye that Keith could scarcely keep a straight face, and she quickly looked away so he wouldn't get her started on a case of the giggles.

Ann turned red. "Oh, no reason. We were just wondering." She shot a nervous glance behind her and then eyed Keith and Char in helpless dismay, as if wishing she could make them disappear. Char knew the feeling. She wanted Ann and Fred to disappear.

"Come on, Ann, let's dance," Fred said impatiently, giving his date's tanned shoulders a possessive squeeze.

"Now, there's a good idea," said Keith. "Let's all dance."

He was already turning to Char when Ann gave a desperate gulp and forced her mouth into an anguished smile. "Gosh, Mr. Webb, how nice of you to ask!" she exclaimed, and thrust herself stiffly into his arms.

"Well, I'll be!" Fred let out an enraged bellow as Ann determinedly steered her astounded partner toward the other side of the dance floor. "I'm gonna kill that guy!"

Char could relate to that. She wanted to kill Ann. She also wanted to jump up and down and scream with disappointment. But she was a mature adult, who didn't want to embarrass Keith by making a scene, so she did none of those things.

Fred was slowly turning purple. "I'm gonna kill him."

Oh, dear. She had to think fast. "I've got a better idea, Fred. Why don't you and I dance?"

"Why should we?"

"Maybe it'll make Ann jealous," she improvised quickly.

Fred gave her a doubtful look that wasn't at all flattering. "I suppose it's worth a try." He put his beefy arm around her and swung her out onto the floor, moving jerkily, out of rhythm with the music.

Keith had better appreciate the sacrifice she was making to save his life, Char thought darkly as Fred stepped on her foot for the third time.

Two seconds later she spotted Ann and Keith. It didn't improve her temper one iota to note that Ann now seemed to be having the time of her life. Who wouldn't be, with Keith for a partner?

Though Ann must have shanghaied him in the first place only as an act of self-sacrifice for Debbie's sake, she certainly wasn't acting like a martyr now! Neither was Keith. Just then he smiled and bent his head to say something that caused Ann to flush prettily and break into animated laughter.

"Ow! Watch your claws, lady," Fred protested as Char's nails dug into him.

"Sorry." Char sighed. She knew dancing with Ann hadn't been Keith's idea, but did he have to act as if he were enjoying it so much? She told herself he was just making the best of an awkward situation, but that didn't make her feel much better. Especially not when Fred trod on her toes again.

Gazing miserably at the throng of couples swirling past them, her eyes focused in recognition on the back of Steve Benson's sandy head. But as the dance brought him closer and he turned slightly, she almost decided she'd been mistaken, because the expression on his face was totally unfamiliar. For once, he wasn't scowling. He was gazing down at his partner with a look that was both dazzled and tender, exalted and tormented.

He's in love. Char recognized it instinctively, and then wondered how she knew. *Because I feel the same way about Keith!* she answered herself, stunned. The knowledge ripped through her like a bolt of lightning. *I'm in love with Keith.* She shut her eyes and took three deep breaths. She was not—repeat, *not*—going to faint on top of Fred.

"Hey, lady, are you all right?" he asked, peering down at her.

"Yes, I'm fine." She didn't want to think about her new discovery. It was too overwhelming. Too scary. And she couldn't face Keith yet. He might read the new emotion in her eyes, and she wasn't ready for that. Not yet.

She looked across the floor at Steve again, and felt a lump in her throat as she recognized the pure, hopeless longing on his tense, boyish face. Taking a look at the young woman in his arms, she could scarcely blame him. The girl was exquisite. Light and fragile as a butterfly, with a cloud of silvery blond hair that curled around her heart-shaped face. Her small white hand clung to Steve's arm as if for support, and her brown eyes were so huge and bright they might have been shimmering with unshed tears.

"Who's that girl Steve's dancing with?" she asked Fred.

"You mean you don't *know?*" He looked at Char as if she were the dumbest person he'd ever met. "That's Debbie."

Eight

"*That's* Debbie? But—" And then she noticed the barely perceptible hesitation as the girl shifted her weight to her left leg. The hint of a limp was so slight that Char had missed it entirely until then.

She took a deep, shaky breath. So *that* was Debbie. Now, at last, Char felt she understood what made Debbie's friends so fiercely loyal and protective. She understood why Keith had gone to such crazy, convoluted lengths to avoid hurting Debbie. How could you bear to hurt someone so young, so desperately vulnerable? How could you be the one to hurl the stone that might shatter her like a pane of glass?

Oh, Keith, she thought, feeling a warm wave of new sympathy for his predicament. He was such a tender, caring, responsible man. That was why they were mixed up together in this situation. And it was one more reason why she couldn't stop herself from loving him.

Keith wasn't hard to spot in a crowd. His height, his raven-black hair, and that lean, gorgeous face of his drew her eyes like a magnet drawing steel.

But she hadn't expected to find him also looking for *her*, and her heart skipped two beats as his fierce gaze locked with hers across the dance floor.

She forgot her own preoccupations as she read the urgent message in his eyes: *"Help!"* With one horrified glance, she saw the reason for his SOS—Ann was skillfully maneuvering him toward Steve and Debbie! Short of engaging his partner in a wrestling match that would have embarrassed everybody, he couldn't do much about it.

But there *was* something Char could do—get Fred over there on the double and cut in on Keith and Ann. Unfortunately, trying to move Fred across the floor was like trying to drive a Mack truck without power steering. To make matters worse, he possessed neither Keith's instinctive chivalry nor Keith's reluctance to make an embarrassing scene.

"Hey, lady, what's the big idea? *I'm* supposed to lead," he loudly informed her.

"But if we—" And then she saw that it was too late. The two couples had reached their rendezvous. Char watched helplessly as Ann, blushing red as a beet, cut in on Steve and Debbie, who both looked pale as ghosts. Keith alone kept his normal color and his cool. He beckoned Debbie into his arms with a friendly smile and a casual nod, as if switching partners had been his own idea.

He was doing his best to pretend that everything was fine and ordinary. But it wasn't going to work if Debbie didn't stop shaking like a leaf. The girl looked ready to faint or burst into tears. It also wouldn't help his act any if Char followed her instincts and barged over there like a jealous witch to yank him away from Debbie.

Inspiration hit just as she was ready to give up. There *was* a way. But it would take some fast talking. And some luck.

"Quick, Fred! Now's your chance to get Ann back! Let's cut in while she's dancing with her brother."

No sooner said than done. After charging toward his goal with all the finesse of a water buffalo, Fred elbowed Steve out of the way, thrust Char at him, and grabbed Ann by the shoulders. "You're coming with me, kid," he growled.

Ann seemed happy to do just that, which left Char face-to-face with Steve Benson. Oh, dear. He was scowling again, and his arms were rigid as he got ready to go through the motions of dancing with her. Damn, this wasn't going to be easy. But her whole plan depended on winning Steve's trust and persuading him to help her. *Here goes nothing*, she thought.

"Congratulations on your scholarship."

Steve gave a hostile shrug.

So much for small talk. "Are you in love with Debbie?" she asked, deciding there was no point in beating around the bush.

He went first red and then absolutely white, but didn't say a word.

Char spoke very gently. "I saw the way you were looking at her tonight."

His scowl grew even fiercer. "So?"

"So I think you *are* in love with her."

"Dammit, what gives you the right to poke your nose into my business?"

"You and your sisters have been trying to interfere in my relationship with Keith Webb. You've been poking your noses into *my* business. What gave *you* that right?"

He flushed and evaded the question. "You don't belong here. The sooner you realize that and go away, the better for everyone."

"For *everyone*, Steve? What about you? Will it

really be better for you if Keith and Debbie end up together?"

He squeezed his eyes shut and spoke through clenched teeth. "I just want her to be happy. She deserves to be happy. She's suffered enough. Can't you understand that?"

"I understand. But Keith won't make her happy, you know."

"He's what she wants," Steve insisted. "She *loves* him."

"Maybe. But he doesn't love *her*. And they're not right for each other! Don't you see? He needs someone who'll stand up to him and spit in his eye and tell him he's full of beans!" *Someone like me*, Char thought fiercely. *He needs me!* "And Debbie needs someone who'll give her the kind of love she's been yearning for. She needs *you*, Steve."

"Me?" He gave a harsh laugh. "She'll never look at me."

"I think she will. Once she realizes she can't have Keith, she'll get over her infatuation, and she'll be ready for a love that's real. It's only natural she'll turn to you, the man she's been leaning on all along."

"You really think that?"

"Yes. But it's not likely to happen if you keep encouraging her to hope that Keith will have a change of heart."

She thought she was getting through to him, but with Steve it was hard to tell. And she was running out of time. One quick glance at Keith and Debbie told her that.

"Think about it," she urged him. "But for now, won't you please help me rescue Debbie?"

"What?" His gaze followed the faint jerk of Char's head. "My God! She's crying."

So she was. But Char saw only Keith's fixed, ghastly smile and the desperation in his green eyes. "We've got to cut in on them. *Now!*" she whispered urgently.

"You're right." Without another word, Steve waltzed her across the floor and tapped on Keith's shoulder. The switch was made without missing a beat.

"Thank God!" Keith murmured hoarsely, straining Char's body close against his as if he could never get enough of the feel of her. His breathing was so deep and ragged, he sounded like a man who'd just run a long-distance race . . . or wakened from a nightmare.

When he drew back far enough to gaze down at her, his face looked strangely haggard. "You saved my life, goddess," he whispered.

"I know."

He brought her close again, and nestled his face against her hair. "I suppose you think I'm over-reacting, but it just tears me up inside to see someone hurting because of *me*, when there's not a damn thing I can do to help."

"I know, love. I know. It wasn't your fault." She reached up and caressed the lean, hard line of his cheek. Her hands slid to the back of his neck beneath his white dinner jacket and began a soothing massage of the tautly corded muscles there.

"Damn that Ann Benson!" he said. "What she needs is a good spanking! Did she think she was doing Debbie any favors tonight, putting her on the spot that way? The poor kid was so mortified at being shoved at me that—*wait a minute*." He stopped abruptly and stared at Char. His eyes and his voice went velvety-soft. "*What* did you call me, just now?"

"I forget." *Oh, Char, you coward*, she inwardly reproached herself.

"You called me 'love.' "

"Um . . . yes, I guess I did," she confessed, lowering her gaze to the top button of his snowy-white shirt.

He smiled down at her. "I'm glad. You're the first person ever to call me that." He sighed. "But now I suppose you're going to tell me not to let it go to my head."

Not trusting herself to speak, she shook her head.

"Does that mean no, you're *not* going to tell me that, or no, I *shouldn't* let it go to my head?"

She lifted her chin and gave him a look of exasperation. "What it means, buster, is stop talking so much and let's dance!"

The chuckle that rumbled deep inside him sent out vibrations that moved from his flesh to hers wherever their bodies touched. Char gasped softly as her breasts shared the motion of his chest when it contracted and spasmed with his laughter. The intimacy of the sensation was indescribable, and she found herself imagining how Keith might move and quicken against her in that same way at the climax of their lovemaking. The thought left her weak as a newborn kitten.

"Oh, goddess," Keith whispered huskily. "How can you expect me to behave myself when you call me 'love' and then look at me like *that*?"

His gaze never left her face as his hands caressed the small of her back in time to the pulsing, sensuous beat of the music. Her hips, rocking gently to the rhythm of the dance, were suddenly urged into intimate contact with his thighs. The fine-woven dark fabric of his trousers rubbed against the dark blue silk of her dress, and Char closed her eyes in an agony of delight as she felt the bold presence of his masculine arousal through the thin layers of cloth.

"I don't know what I expect anymore," she confessed breathlessly, punctuating her words with a tongue-tipped kiss on the smooth bronzed skin of his throat. Everything seemed to have changed the minute she realized she loved him.

Keith groaned. "You're not helping me here, Char. You'd better get tough, or we're going to disgrace ourselves in front of this whole crowd."

"But I don't *feel* tough." In fact, she felt soft and liquid inside, like the center of a chocolate-covered cherry candy.

Grimacing, Keith lifted his hand to trace the line of her slim white neck. "You're right, dammit. You don't feel tough at all. Just satiny-soft and warm . . ." His fingers, like whispers of desire, brushed her bare shoulders, and then stilled. He sighed. "What am I going to do with you, goddess?"

"Take me home?" she suggested recklessly. Oh, dear. The instant the words were out of her mouth, she wanted to call them back. Being in love was making her crazy, she thought. "Um, that is—"

"Sure," Keith said, breathing deeply and staring down at her in astonished delight. "I'll take you home right now."

"But I—"

He was already leading her off the dance floor. "Wait here while I get your wrap," he said when they reached a park bench at the outer edge of the crowd. "You left it at our table, right?"

"Yes, but—" He was gone. Damn. What was she going to do? How could she rescind the blatant sexual invitation she'd given him? And did she really *want* to rescind it? Lord knows, she'd meant every word. There was nothing she wanted more than to go home with him and share his bed and love every square inch of his magnificent body, all night long. She wanted to give him all the love that was exploding inside her. But . . .

"Ms. Smith." The young, resolute voice behind

her made Char jump. She turned and found herself face-to-face with Debbie, who looked pale and determined. "We need to talk," the younger woman said quietly.

"Yes?" Char was the one who sounded nervous.

"I want you to know, Ms. Smith, you've done me a big favor."

"I have?" Well, of course she had, she thought. That was what the whole charade had been about—helping Debbie. But how could Debbie know that?

"I'm sure you never intended it, Ms. Smith, but you've given me hope. Does that surprise you?"

"Well, uh . . ."

"You see, before I met you, I didn't believe you existed. I was sure Keith was just making you up! And I thought he'd dumped me because of something lacking in *me*. I thought I'd lost him because of my own inadequacies." Debbie lifted her chin, and her whole face seemed to radiate a newfound confidence. "Now I know that's not true."

"I see," Char said cautiously. *Thank God!* she wanted to shout. *Keith and I have done some good for her after all. She's going to be all right!*

But Debbie wasn't finished yet.

"Now I know it wasn't a case of my losing Keith, but of your *stealing* him!" she accused Char. "But I'm warning you right now, I intend to get him back."

"What?" Char couldn't believe her ears. Was this the same shrinking violet who'd looked ready to break into little pieces earlier? One thing was certain—when Debbie Forrest decided to get her confidence back and take a positive approach, she didn't mess around.

"Oh, sure, he's infatuated with you now," Debbie said, "but how long do you expect it to last? I'll bet you're not even planning to stay on in Webb Falls, are you? You'll go as soon as your assignment here is finished, because your job is more important to you than being with Keith. But *I'll* still be here, waiting for him to get tired of his long-distance love affair with a woman who'd rather race all over the map than share his life."

Char frowned, barely registering the fact that Debbie must have been checking up on her pretty thoroughly. She didn't want to have to think about the problems Debbie was pointing out. Not yet. She wasn't ready! Somehow she'd tumbled into love with Keith W. Webb, and now she needed time to adjust to *that* mind-boggling fact before she started worrying about the future. She didn't even know yet if Keith loved her! If he did, there'd be time enough later to agonize over whether the demands of her job might come between them.

"Keith and I will cross that bridge when we come to it," she said aloud.

"And I'll be waiting on the other side," said Debbie. She sounded so sure of herself that Char felt an involuntary chill.

Just then Keith stepped out of the shadows, carrying Char's wrap. "I had to look all over for this—" He broke off abruptly when he caught sight of Debbie.

"I was just leaving," Debbie said quickly. "But don't forget what I told you, Ms. Smith." She walked away without a backward glance.

"What was that all about?" Keith asked, looking troubled.

Char sighed. "She just wanted me to know she hasn't given up on you yet."

"She's nuts. Can't she see I've got eyes for nobody but you?" He stepped up behind her and draped the silky wrap over her bare shoulders, letting his hands linger in a seductive caress of her upper arms.

"But she said—"

"Never mind what she said. Let's forget about her and everybody else in this town. Because tonight is for *us*, goddess. Just you and me."

His words held a promise her heart could not resist. *Tonight is for us.* She wanted that night with him, the man she loved, more than she'd ever wanted anything. She wanted to taste the sweet, fiery magic they could make together. Nothing else seemed important anymore.

She shivered in eager response as his arms wrapped around her from behind, drawing her snugly against him. Her eyes closed as she relished the feel of his forearms cradling the rounded weight of her breasts. He kissed the hollow behind her ear and then the nape of her neck. Each touch of his lips sent flame-tipped arrows of desire arcing through her.

"I'm ready whenever you are," she murmured. "To leave, that is," she quickly added, in case he got the wrong idea.

Keith chuckled at her hasty clarification. Once again Char felt her own body gently rocked by the vibrations of his laughter. Her breasts, unbound beneath the low-cut silk of her dress, jiggled against his forearm. She knew by his quick indrawn breath that he could feel her nipples hardening, pressing like tiny pebbles against his arm.

"I'm ready, too, goddess. So very ready." Nestled in the hard cradle of his hips, she could feel how ready he was. "Let's go," he said.

They walked to the car. Char felt the sounds and scents of the summer night with a sharp, indelible clarity. She would always remember this night— the smell of the cool breeze from the woods and the river, the pale wedge of moon in the sky, the swaying colored lanterns strung along the path, the sound of dance music fading behind them. She clung to the man beside her, reassured by the muscled warmth and bulk of him that this was no dream, though it felt like one.

In the car, Keith started the engine and headed out of town. Char recognized the road to his house from her previous trip. The scent of new-mown hay was sweet and heavy on the air that blew through the open windows, cooling her flushed cheeks. This was really happening, she told herself. *I'm going to make love with Keith tonight.*

"Why tonight?" Keith's question came out of the blue, startling her because it sounded uncannily like a response to her unspoken thought.

"What?"

"Tonight . . . something changed," he said slowly. "I think your feelings about *me* must have changed. And I'm sure not complaining, but I'd like to know why."

"Oh." She felt panic. No way did she have the guts to come right out and say, "Tonight I realized I'm in love with you." She just couldn't reveal herself to him that fully when she didn't know what his feelings were.

"Is that all you've got to say? Just 'oh'?" He sounded amused, but she got the impression that he wouldn't give up asking until she'd given him an answer.

"My image of you changed when I found out how much you'd done for the hospital, and when you got up and announced the scholarship," she said stiffly. Oh, dear, she thought, she must sound like a Goody Two-Shoes. She tried again. "It was seeing what you represented to the people of Webb Falls . . ." But that sounded even worse. He might get the idea that she'd been impressed by his wealth and high social position in the community, which wasn't what she meant at all!

"You're kidding, right?" The tension in his voice was palpable. "Please tell me you're kidding?"

"No, not exactly kidding," Char said nervously. "But I didn't explain it very well. You see—"

"Oh, I think you explained it just fine!" Keith broke in bitterly. "What it boils down to is, you decided you're willing to sleep with me because I'm such a solid, respectable *pillar* of the community! Hell, if I'd known *that* was all it took to get into your bed—"

"Shut up! That's not true and you know it!" Her throat tightened with gathering sobs. She couldn't understand what was happening. One minute they were lovers on their way home to be truly together at last, and now they were like two cats screeching at each other just before lashing out with claws and teeth.

With a wrench of the wheel, Keith steered the car onto the shoulder of the road and braked to a jolting stop on the rough surface.

"Why are we stopping?"

"Because you and I are going to talk. And I'm much too angry to drive and talk at the same time. Besides," he added sardonically, "there's not much point in trying to reach our original destination, is there? I don't know about you, but I've certainly lost the mood."

"That makes two of us!" She only wished it were true. Though she was angry, confused, and hurt by his insulting remarks, she hadn't 'lost the mood.' She still wanted him with a passion that sizzled through her like heat lightning through a sultry sky.

Char took a deep, steadying breath. She needed to get a grip on her volatile emotions so she could find out why Keith was acting this way.

"Why are you so angry with me?" she asked in a calm, curious voice. "I know I made a stupidly inarticulate remark, which you misinterpreted. But I don't understand why you flew into a rage over it. It doesn't make sense."

Keith expelled a long, pent-up sigh. "You're right. It doesn't make sense for me to get angry with you for not being the woman I thought you were. The mistake was mine, not yours."

"*What* mistake? What kind of woman did you think I was, for heaven's sake?"

"I thought you were different, Char—someone who could share the laughter, the magic, the special little things in life that mean so much. When I looked into your eyes, I thought I saw dreams and hopes that matched my own. So I opened up to you. With you, I felt I could be myself, let my imagination run free. You brought out a part of me I've tended to hide from others—my playful, romantic side."

"*What?*" She couldn't believe her ears. Right from the start, he'd bowled her over with his mischievous, irresistible charm. She'd been so bewitched by it, yet so distrustful. And now he made it sound as if that fanciful inventiveness were a very private facet of his personality. Something he'd shared only with her. "You mean to tell me the way you act around me isn't the way you usually act?" she demanded.

"Of course it's not. How could it be? Until recently, my life was full to the brim with ambitions, business decisions, challenges, and responsibilities. But part of me was getting lost in the shuffle. Luckily, moving out to the farm helped change that. And then . . . I met you. You seemed like a dream come true."

"And now you think you were wrong about me?" That hurt.

"Hell, yes. What you responded to tonight was the conventional, superficial, public side of Keith

Webb—the man who shakes hands, writes checks, and says the things he's supposed to say. *That's* what turns you on! You couldn't care less about the real me!"

Char had to laugh. "That is a crock of . . . sauerkraut! Of course it's 'the real you' I care about, you big jerk! Unless you're trying to tell me that you contributed to the hospital, started up a scholarship fund, and practically bent over backward and did jumping jacks to avoid hurting Debbie Forrest, all for the sake of your *image*, without giving a damn about the people involved?"

"Well, no, but—"

"I didn't think so. And I don't think there's anything wrong with my responding to the compassionate, caring side of you, either. Why shouldn't it matter to me that you care about people?"

There was a long moment of silence. Char wished she could see Keith's face, but the car's interior was almost pitch black.

"Damn," he said at last. "I've been acting like a crazy person. I don't know what got into me, Char. I'm sorry."

"Consider yourself forgiven. And, Keith . . ." She hesitated, feeling she owed him a deeper explanation about why her feelings toward him had changed, even if that explanation got him mad at her all over again. "There's something you ought to know about me." She reached out her hand to touch his shoulder, and followed the taut line of his arm to where his hand still gripped the steering wheel.

"I'm listening, Char." His hand released the wheel and turned, open-palmed, to accept her hand in a warm, comforting clasp. That reassuring link between them made it so much easier to begin.

"When I was a little girl, I knew a charming,

handsome man who could always make me laugh. He enchanted me with his elaborate stories and extravagant compliments. But as time went by, I found out the hard way that I couldn't depend on him or anything he said. That man was my father." She felt Keith's hand suddenly clench around hers. "When he left us for the last time, it was just one more betrayal out of many."

Keith's fingers were gripping hers so hard it was almost painful, but she welcomed the fierce pressure of flesh on flesh. It told her he was listening, caring, responding.

"That experience left its mark," she went on. "I'm not very trusting when it comes to men. Especially not charming, witty, romantic, terribly good-looking men who try to sweep me off my feet." She smiled. "Well, recently I met a man who was all that, and more."

Keith snorted disgustedly. "If you mean me—"

"Hush up and let me finish my story. By the way, I forgot to mention that this guy is *very* conceited. He has an ego the size of Texas."

"Dammit, Char—"

"I said *hush*. Right away, this guy and I 'clicked.' We communicated, we shared, we laughed together, and every time we touched, it was like magic. I couldn't help liking him, wanting him, caring for him. But I didn't trust my own feelings, and I didn't trust him. Because I was scared to death of falling for a man who might be like my father."

"But—"

"Hold your horses, Webb. I'm almost through. One night, I finally realized he wasn't just another fast talker with a pretty face." She grinned mischievously. "Not only was he a genuine *philanthropist*, but also a solid, respectable *pillar* of his community! And he—*ouch!*"

"I didn't pinch you *that* hard," he said indignantly.

"*I'll* be the judge of that," she said, laughing as she rubbed the spot just under her ribs where his nimble fingers had attacked. "You don't know your own strength."

"Want me to kiss it and make it better?"

"Hmm, that's not a bad idea."

She caught her breath as she heard and felt him moving beside her in the darkness. And then she gasped, because her head and shoulders were falling backward at a dizzying speed as he moved the lever that tilted her seat into a reclining position.

He adjusted his own seat, and then leaned over her. "Let me just get my bearings here a sec," he said huskily, running his hand up along her silk-clad body from knee to shoulders.

"But you didn't pinch me *there*," Char said breathlessly, as his hand lingered on her breast.

"My mistake. Lower, goddess?"

"Huh? Oh, right. Lower."

His hand moved to her thighs, caressing her with slow, seductive strokes. "Here, goddess?"

"Mmm, ye—I mean no. A little higher than that."

"Maybe you'd better show me."

Her hand was shaking as she guided his palm to her rib cage, and she felt a leap of fire in her loins when his knuckles brushed the undersides of her breasts. Then he bent his head to bestow the promised kiss of healing, and the sweet pressure of his lips warmed her skin even through the fabric of her dress.

"That's the spot," she murmured, running her fingers through his silky, tousled hair. His clean-shaven cheek was within millimeters of her breast, and it was only a matter of seconds before he turned his head to nuzzle her bosom.

His kisses climbed to the low-cut neckline of her

dress and then explored beneath the layer of silk, seeking out her nipples, circling and wetting them with his tongue. Char's throaty cry signaled how intense the pleasure was that he gave her.

And then, as if her voice had called him there, he lifted his mouth to hers, fitting lip to lip and tongue to tongue in a passionate kiss that exploded with need and desire. When they had to stop to find breath, they clung to each other, panting softly.

"Oh, goddess," Keith whispered. "How could I have doubted this magic we give to each other?"

Char wasn't sure he expected an answer, but she decided to offer him one. "Sometimes it's hard to believe in magic. Too often it turns out to be an illusion—a trick done with mirrors. That's why you can only trust in the magic once you trust the magician."

Keith was silent a minute, and when he spoke, his voice was thoughtful. "And that's why your feelings toward me changed tonight, isn't it? Tonight you found out I was the kind of man you felt you could trust, so you finally let yourself believe in our magic."

"Yes. I'm sorry it was so difficult for me to realize the obvious, but—"

"I understand, Char. I only wish I'd guessed that you needed that kind of reassurance. I've gotten so used to people automatically assuming they can rely on me."

"And not without reason. They know you're a man who keeps his promises and lives up to his responsibilities." She brought her lips close to his ear and whispered huskily, "But do they know you're an irresistible, incurable romantic? Not to mention impossibly sexy?"

"Not if you haven't told them."

"Then my lips are sealed. It'll be our secret." Not

that his sexiness would be a secret to any woman who had eyes in her head, Char thought. And then she was too busy responding to his kisses to think anymore.

"Hmm, your lips don't feel sealed to me," he said shakily, after he'd thoroughly and sensuously explored her mouth with his own lips and tongue.

"Never to you," she vowed.

The silence between them was intimate and warm as Keith started the car and pulled onto the road again. Char felt a profound joy in the deeper understanding they had reached following their quarrel. She knew their lovemaking that night would bring their bodies together in a magical expression of the union that already existed in their hearts. Even though Keith hadn't said in so many words that he loved her, she felt an ever-growing certainty that he did.

And then the car slowed. Keith pulled onto the shoulder again. He turned to face Char in the darkness, and when he spoke, his voice was taut with pain and determination. "We can't do this," he said. "It would be a terrible mistake."

Nine

"Well, not a *terrible* mistake, exactly," he corrected himself when Char's only response was a devastated silence, "Hell, it would be the most divinely satisfying mistake we'd ever make! But still a mistake, Char."

"How can you say that?"

"Because of what you told me tonight. You're counting on me to live up to my responsibilities and keep my promises. And it suddenly hit me that I made one very important promise to you about *us*—that we wouldn't get involved like this so long as I was your client!"

"Oh. But that was . . . I've changed my mind. It doesn't matter anymore."

"I think it does. Your professional ethics may seem unimportant to you tonight, but what about tomorrow? I think I know you pretty well, Char. Aren't you likely to have strong regrets about not living up to your own standard of what's right?"

"I suppose it's possible," she admitted dully, knowing down deep that he was right. Damn. She didn't want to think about tomorrow—she wanted

Keith, and she wanted him tonight. "But it's my own choice to make, and I say—"

"No, Char. I've been pretty irresponsible up to now, letting myself get carried away by my feelings for you, and doing my damnedest to tempt you into getting carried away along with me! But no more. From now on, I am Mr. Responsible, and that means that you and I are not going to make love until our professional relationship as client and consultant is officially over."

"Damn!" Char exclaimed. "Me and my big mouth! I don't *want* you to be responsible right now, Keith! I want you to kiss me and touch me and take me to bed."

He groaned. "Don't make this any tougher for me than it already is," he pleaded. "I want us to start off right, Char. Surely that's worth waiting for."

After a long moment of silent struggle, she found the strength to painfully relinquish, for a few days, the delights they had come so close to sharing. "Yes, it's worth waiting for," she said.

Keith turned the car around and headed back toward town. He was right, Char knew, but that didn't mean she'd ever forgive him for it! At the same time, she appreciated the strength and *caring* it must have taken for him to make his decision. And that made her love him all the more.

When they reached the Benson place, she leaned over to drop one fleeting kiss on his taut cheek. That was all either of them could risk. "Don't walk me to the door," she said. "Because I hate long good-byes. And I promise you, as soon as this consulting project is completed, I'll be in the mood for one heck of a celebration . . . with you."

"I'm counting on it, goddess."

She got out and walked to the Bensons' front porch before turning to wave good night. When he drove away, she watched as his taillights grew smaller in the distance, blurring to look like red blossoms behind the tears in her eyes.

"Cha-ar! Pho-one!" Lisa Benson's healthy twelve-year-old lungs emitted a shout that would have carried up six flights of stairs, let alone just the one.

Char leaped out of the tub, where she'd been luxuriating in a froth of scented bubbles, soaking away the strains and stresses of working nonstop for ten days to complete the consulting project ahead of schedule. Hardly taking time to towel herself dry, she threw on her dark blue quilted robe and rushed to the top of the stairs.

"Is it Keith?" she asked breathlessly. If *anything* had come up to interfere with the night they had planned, she was going to scream and hold her breath until she turned blue.

"Nah," said Lisa. "But I think it's long distance."

That must mean it was an emergency, because nobody outside Webb Falls knew her phone number here. Someone had gone to a lot of trouble to reach her. Immediately Char thought of Pippi and the baby, and she blamed herself for not finding time to get in touch with her family during the past couple of weeks. Never mind that she'd been working eighteen-hour days—she could at least have managed a two-minute phone call!

Her fingers shook as she picked up the receiver. "Hello?"

"Char? This is Arri."

The minute Char heard her middle sister Arrietty's tear-choked voice, she was sure that all her worst fears were about to be confirmed. "Arri! What is it? Is it Pippi?"

"Pippi? Of course not. It's John. He's broken our engagement."

"Thank God!" Char exclaimed in relief. "That is, I'm sorry about your engagement, but—"

"He said I was *boring*, Char. And the longer I sit here alone with this box of Kleenex, staring at the walls of my apartment, thinking about my life—" Her voice broke. "I'm afraid he's right."

"Nonsense!" Everything else faded from Char's mind as she responded to her sister's cry for help. "I've known you all your life, and I say you're not one bit boring! And John Dover is a fine one to talk. He seemed like an okay guy, but frankly, he had all the personality of a bowl of cream of wheat! I never figured out what you saw in him."

Arri sobbed again. "But don't you see? That *proves* I'm boring, because I picked him to fall in love with. I wanted someone safe and sensible and predictable, who wouldn't let me down. And now he's dumped me for a girl with purple hair who rides a Harley and teaches aerobic dancing!"

"*Purple* hair? Oh, Arri, I'm so sorry." Her thoughts targeted on what her sister had just said about picking John because he was safe and sensible. She sighed. "It occurs to me that you and I have both been making the same mistake."

"What mistake?"

"We've both tried so hard not to get tangled up with men like our father that we've ended up going to the opposite extremes. Until now, I've never let myself fall for *any* man at all! And you fell for a man who's so shallow and unimaginative, he judges a woman's personality by her hair color! Of course you're not boring, but John never had enough depth to appreciate how complex and fascinating you really are."

"Oh, sure. Right now I feel about as complex and fascinating as Saran Wrap."

Ignoring this bit of defeatism, Char went on expounding her own thoughts. "You don't need a man who's *safe*—you need one who makes you feel special and extraordinary." *The way Keith makes me feel*, she thought.

"Don't tell me what kind of man I need," Arri wailed. "Just tell me how to stop hurting over this one. How do I stop feeling like a loser who's so dull I might as well be in a coma?"

"Hmm. I haven't discovered any new cures for a broken heart. All I can give you are the old standbys—time, work, friends, new interests, new scenery, a new love. Anything that gets you feeling good about yourself or starts you thinking about something or someone besides yourself."

"But my life is so boring, there's *nothing* to take my mind off myself or to feel good about!"

"Baloney!" Char snapped impatiently. "If you really believe that, then *change* your life! Why not ask for a month's leave from the library and take that trip to Europe you keep dreaming about? Do it *now*! I'll be glad to help pay the fare. Or you could take up a new hobby or sport. Volunteer for something. But just quit—"

"Feeling sorry for myself?" Arri wryly finished the sentence. "You're right, Char. It's up to me to make my life what I want it to be." She paused. "You know, I think I *will* take that trip. I'll buy the ticket first thing tomorrow! And if it's the last thing I ever do, I'm going to prove that John Dover was an idiot to dump me! I *refuse* to be boring."

"Bravo! And maybe while you're in Europe you'll meet a man who'll make you forget all about John."

Arri gave a doubting laugh. "I swear, Char, you've got romance on the brain! But you've really helped me see the light. Thanks for everything."

"That's what sisters are for." After all, she thought as she said her good-byes and hung up, it was only a couple of weeks ago that her other sister, Pippi, had helped *her* see the light about her fears of making a commitment to a man. And realizing that had been the first step in recognizing her love for Keith.

Tonight was going to be another big step for them. She and Keith would become lovers at last. But that was just the beginning . . . she hoped. Would he tell her he loved her? And if he did, what then? What about the future?

The sun was going down as she drove up the gravel drive to Keith's farmhouse on the hill. It was a hot, sultry evening, and thunderheads were gathering on the western horizon, creating a blazing sunset of spectacular reds and purples.

Char stepped out of the car and took a deep breath of the scented country air. She wore a ruffled, romantic, off-the-shoulder sundress of cool white eyelet cotton. Her auburn hair flowed loose down her back, glowing like fire where it caught the light of the sunset.

She turned toward the house and felt the air whoosh out of her lungs at the sight of Keith standing on the porch, watching her. He looked cool, dark, and exciting in a yellow polo shirt and khaki hiking shorts. For one long, electric moment they exchanged glances, and then Keith started down the porch steps and Char ran across the grass to meet him.

They went into each other's arms as naturally as breathing, and with the same urgent need. For a long time they just held each other, hardly daring to believe they were together at last.

"The waiting's been hell, Char," Keith whispered against the flower-scented softness of her hair. "And now you look and feel even more beautiful than I remembered."

"Irregular meals and lack of sleep must agree

with me, then," she said shakily. She knew that, by rights, she should have been haggard and hollow-eyed after her single-minded marathon of work to finish the project. Instead, tonight she was blooming with love and excitement.

"Damn, I've hated to see you pushing yourself so hard. You'll never know how many times I came *that close* to barging into your office at midnight and saying, 'The hell with waiting!' "

"I'm glad I *didn't* know, or I might have been the one doing the barging! But now that it's over, I'm glad we waited. I think this report may be the best work I've ever done, and I wouldn't want anything to tarnish that." What she left unsaid was that she didn't want anything to tarnish their loving, either. At the moment it didn't seem possible that anything *could*.

"You've got a right to be proud of the work you've done. You sure impressed the committee! After the briefing you gave today, they voted unanimously to go with your recommendations."

Char permitted herself one small sigh of relief and satisfaction. "I'm glad," she said simply. "But now let's forget about all that. Our *official* involvement is over. From now on, it's strictly personal."

"Very personal," he huskily agreed, tightening his tanned, taut-muscled arms around her. One hand caressed her smooth bare shoulder and the other clasped her slender waist. She was like a fragrant white gardenia cupped between his palms.

Then, without warning, he swept her up in his arms and started walking toward the house.

"Ohh! Mmm." Char sighed in delicious excitement. "May I ask what you're doing?" Whatever it was, she loved it.

"Can't you guess? I'm carrying you off into the sunset."

Her eyes flew open in alarm. "That doesn't mean

I have to get up on a horse, does it? I'm really not wild about being thrown across anyone's saddle—not even yours."

He laughed. "We won't need a horse to get us where we're going tonight, goddess."

"Good." She closed her eyes again and smiled a secret smile of anticipation. The sound of Keith's footsteps crossing the porch was like a theatrical drum roll before the curtain rose on a play. He opened the door and started up the stairs, two at a time. "What strong lungs and thighs you must have," she murmured against his ear.

"The better to love you with," he growled softly, in imitation of the big bad wolf.

Char gazed up at him with questioning eyes. Just by using that one little word—"love"—even in jest, he'd taken her breath away. How she hoped he meant it!

Keith carried her down the hall to his bedroom, where warm, rose-colored light flooded in from the setting sun. Lowering her to the bed, he leaned over her and looked deep into her vulnerable blue eyes. "Shall I tell you how you make me feel, goddess?"

Her heart beat so hard, she imagined it might drown out her reply. "Only if it's what I want to hear," she said in a weak attempt at humor.

"I can't promise you that."

"No?" She felt her heart plummet. Did he mean that he didn't love her? she wondered. "You'd better tell me anyway," she said in what was meant to be a firm, calm voice.

"I *hope* it's what you want to hear." He gave her a sober, searching look. "I'm head over heels in love with you, Char. You make me feel that I've rediscovered myself, all because of loving you."

Char stared up at him, feeling her eyes grow moist and a lump form in her throat. "Why the hell wouldn't I want to hear *that*, you big ape?" she demanded in a choked voice. With an unromantic sniffle, she flung her arms around his neck and pulled him down on top of her. "Don't you know that's exactly how I feel about *you*?"

"It *is*?" A smile of incredible joy lit his face, but a trace of uncertainty lingered.

"I love you, Keith." She lifted her hands to frame the taut, angular planes of his beautiful face, and then urged his head down to hers. Their mouths met in a kiss more magical than any that had gone before, because this time they freely gave their hearts and souls to each other.

Lifting his head to catch his breath, Keith ran his fingers through the bright waves of her hair that spilled like flame-tinted silk across the bed. His hand followed the shining cascade to her shoulder, her arm, her breast. Char moaned softly as his palm circled the place where her taut nipple pressed against the white sundress.

While his hand caressed her, his lips explored the smooth expanse of her shoulders, left bare by the elasticized neckline of the dress. Char thought she would die when the hot pressure of his mouth began to ease the ruffled top down over the fullness of her breasts. She gripped his shoulders, thrilling in their muscled strength even as she tugged against them, trying in vain to speed his lips on their frustratingly slow but erotic journey to where her bared nipples burned for his touch like hard, glowing embers.

And then he was there, suckling her with a hunger that sent heat spiraling between her thighs, making her cry out with wanting more. His seeking hands left the top of her dress hanging loose around her waist and moved on, pulling up her ruffled skirt to find the satiny skin of her inner thighs.

When he touched her through the embroidered silk of her panties, her hips arched in instinctive welcome of his heated caress. He tugged the delicate wisp of fabric down her legs, leaving her naked save for the white ruffles of the dress that tumbled in disarray at her hips.

Char reached out with trembling hands to push his shirt up over his chest and arms, and then Keith quickly pulled it the rest of the way off over his head. His bare torso felt hot to her touch, and his skin glistened with a fine sheen of perspiration as she ran her hands down over his rib cage and his drum-hard belly. When she reached for the snap at the waistband of his shorts, she felt his whole body quiver with tension.

"Let me do it," he said hoarsely. "I'm afraid if you touch me now, I won't be able to wait."

"Wait for what?" she whispered teasingly.

"Until I'm inside you, goddess." He got up off the bed and let his shorts and briefs drop to the floor. The setting sun turned his tanned skin to bronze, and Char felt her breath catch in her throat. The sheer physical beauty of his aroused body was beyond words, and it made her melt like honey to think of him being inside her.

She felt the blood humming in her ears as she rose to her knees and pulled her dress off over her head with slow, deliberate movements. For a long moment she knelt there on the bed, offering her body, gilded with the peach-gold light of the western sky, to the man she loved. Her eyes, blazing with the depths of her passion, met Keith's as he saw her naked for the very first time.

He caught his breath at her loveliness. "Now I *know* you're a goddess," he whispered. "You not only have the power to tame lions, but also the power to make an ordinary man turn wild with wanting you." He sank to the bed and pulled her to him, breathing deep and hard.

"Wait," Char insisted, clasping his forearms and holding their bodies apart for one brief moment more. She smiled. "I can't let you get away with calling yourself an ordinary man. You're not ordinary, Keith."

His eyes darkened with emotion. "Not when I'm with you," he agreed hoarsely. And then he swept her arms aside and brought their bodies so close that she could feel each thudding beat of his heart and each unsteady pant of his breath. Thigh to thigh and breast to breast, their melded flesh shared the same slippery bond of perspiration and the same scorching heat of urgent desire.

Her thighs parted to cradle his hardness and her hips arched in the tender grip of his hands. And then he was inside her, filling her, loving her. It was pure magic. Holding on to each other for dear life, they moved as one in the timeless rhythm of love. Their cries of passion rose to a crescendo as they rocked each other ever closer to the edge of sweet oblivion. And then they were over the brink, catapulted into ecstasy and beyond.

For Char, the journey back from the heights of their lovemaking felt like coming home. Home to the warmth and safety of Keith's arms. She couldn't remember ever feeling so deeply at peace as she did at that moment, lying intimately entwined with him while the last light of the sunset faded from the room, cocooning them in soft-edged darkness.

"Oh, love, you were magnificent," he whispered, stroking her bare back.

Char shook her head, smiling dreamily. "No, I distinctly remember—the magnificent one was *you.*"

"Shall we agree to disagree, goddess?"

Her mouth curved mischievously. "No, I'd rather we put it to the test. The obvious thing to do is to keep making love until we can agree on who's magnificent."

Keith's chuckle was low and sexy. "Sounds good to me," he said. "But I warn you—it'll take forever to change *my* mind."

"Oh, yeah? Well, that goes double for me, buster," Char declared with mock pugnacity, lifting her chin at him and then tucking it against his neck to nuzzle the underside of his clean-shaven jaw.

"*Double* forever?"

"You betcha. You'll *never* convince me you're not magnifi—ohhh." She moaned with pleasure as his hand slipped between her thighs to the silky, tremulous core of her.

"Maybe not. But I'll have one hell of a good time trying," he vowed, and then rained a storm of kisses down her breasts.

"Me too," she murmured fervently. "Me too."

"Now you'll *have* to admit I'm right," Keith drawled in her ear much, much later.

Char felt as if her bones had liquefied into syrup. Her body was limp with the sweetest fatigue she'd ever known. But still she found the energy to disagree. "No, *I'm* right and you're magnificent."

Their soft laughter mingled as they snuggled closer, sharing a wordless contentment. If only they could lie like this forever, Char thought. There *must* be a way to hold fast their love and the magic they'd found together.

But what about her job and the nomadic lifestyle it demanded of her? She knew she could never give up consulting, not even for Keith. After working so hard to achieve expertise and respect in her profession, she couldn't imagine throwing it all away. Besides, she loved the work she did. But how would she bear the constant, prolonged separations from the man she loved? And what would those separations do to Keith's love for her?

"You've gone tense as piano wire." His voice rumbled in her ear, and his hands began a soothing massage of her shoulders and neck. "What's troubling you, goddess?"

She didn't try to evade the question. "I was thinking about my job and my darn travel schedule," she admitted. "I dread the thought of being away from you for weeks at a time, but I don't know what to do about it."

Keith was silent for a long moment, and then his reply left her stunned. "You could ask for a promotion and tell them you want to do less traveling."

"*What?* But Keith, I can't just—"

"Why not? Haven't you paid your dues to that company for the past five years? Isn't it about time they gave you some recognition for the superb work you've done for them?"

"But . . ." Her protest died as she realized the truth of what he'd said. And she remembered that he'd tried to tell her the same thing once before. Brannon-Hale owed her a better deal than she'd been getting, and it was time to stand up for herself and tell them so. The thought was rather scary. "What if they say no?"

"*If* they say no, won't it make sense to think twice about whether you want to go on working for a firm that doesn't value or reward you properly?"

"Are you suggesting . . . that I *quit*?" A fist of panic tightened in her chest at the very thought. Her job with Brannon-Hale gave her financial and emotional security. It meant bills paid on time, money in the bank, and careful investments for a secure, predictable future. It meant never having to lie awake at night feeling the terrible, gnawing fear she'd known as a child when her mother was bravely struggling to keep their little family one step ahead of disaster. And it meant never being financially dependent on anyone who might let her down the way her father had.

Keith gave her a puzzled look. "There *are* other consulting firms, Char. Lots of them. Or you could start your own firm. With your credentials and expertise, I don't doubt you'd be highly successful at it. There are a number of cities within a hundred-mile radius of Webb Falls that you could draw clients from."

He was moving way too fast for her, she realized. She'd barely started to accept the fact that it was time to ask the firm for a better travel schedule, and now he was suggesting she burn her bridges and strike out on her own! No way, she thought.

"I think I'll stick with Brannon-Hale," she said firmly. "After all, I've got five years invested there. And the more I think about it, the more confident I am that they'll be willing to start giving me assignments closer to home. Especially once they see what a crackerjack job I've done for your company."

"That's the spirit." He took her hand and squeezed it tenderly in the darkness. "But whatever happens with your job, we'll find a way to be together. I've got faith in us, goddess."

"Me too." They lapsed into a loving silence, until Char's stomach reminded her that she'd skipped lunch that day because of butterflies over the final briefing on the project. And breakfast had been just toast and coffee on the run. "Keith?"

"Yes?"

"Please understand, I have *no* complaints about the entertainment and hospitality I've been getting as your guest tonight. In my book, you're the host with the *most*. But I do have one small question. Are you planning on feeding me any time soon?"

He tensed. "Damn! I totally forgot about dinner!"

She laughed. "That makes two of us. But now I'm starving."

Keith leaped out of bed and grabbed his pants. "I had everything ready, just sitting in the refrigerator. Lie there and don't move a muscle, and I'll bring it right up."

He was as good as his word. They sat on the rumpled bedspread, drinking Dom Perignon champagne and eating a chilled feast of smoked salmon, pasta salad with shrimp, French bread, cheese, and fresh fruit. After they'd finished stuffing themselves, they set their empty plates on the floor, threw back the covers, and crawled between the sheets together.

Outside, the sultry heat broke at last as the storm clouds moved in from the west. Rain rattled against the windows, and thunder and lightning ripped the sky. Keith and Char scarcely noticed; they were too busy making lightning of their own.

Ten

The phone rang as they were lingering over a late and leisurely breakfast in Keith's sunny kitchen, playing footsie under the oak table.

Keith groaned. "That had better not be the office. I told them I was taking the day off, and I intend to spend it with you even if the whole company falls apart without me! Which it won't," he added modestly.

"Not in one day, anyway," Char agreed with a twinkle in her eye.

But the call wasn't for Keith. "It's Faye," he said, handing the phone to Char. She blushed. Though she'd mentioned to her landlady that she planned to be away for a day or two, she hadn't openly admitted she'd be staying with Keith. It obviously hadn't been too tough to figure out, however.

"Sorry to bother you, dear." Faye sounded flustered. "But your office in Boston is trying to reach you. Somebody at the Webb plant gave them your number here, and I promised I'd do my best to pass along the message. They want you to be in Boston by this afternoon for a talk with your boss."

"*Damn.*" There went her perfect, precious day with Keith. But when the senior partner at Brannon-Hale issued a command, it was wisest to obey. "Guess I'll have to catch a flight out of Albany. And I'll have to stop by the house to change clothes. Did they say what this talk is supposed to be about?"

"No, but I got the impression it's something to do with your work for the Webb Company."

"Maybe they want to promote me," she said cheerfully, trying to ignore the sudden quiver of apprehension that raced along her spine. They *couldn't* have had any complaints about her work, she thought. That just wasn't possible.

"I'll keep my fingers crossed for you, dear," Faye said. "Good-bye and good luck."

"Thanks, Faye. 'Bye." She depressed the button to break the connection, and then started punching in the Boston area code and Brannon-Hale's number as soon as she heard the dial tone.

A few minutes later she hung up, no wiser than before. All they could tell her at the office was to get there on the double. Not why. Not whether to expect good news or bad. But how could it be *bad*? she reasoned. Her work for the Webb Company was probably the best she'd ever done. Still, she couldn't help feeling an uneasy sense of urgency. She *had* to get there right away and find out what this was all about.

Her finger hung poised over the buttons on the telephone as she debated which airline to call for flight information. It was the sound of a chair abruptly scraping the floor behind her that reminded her of Keith's presence.

The look on his face when she turned around was full of anger and hurt that he was desperately trying to control. "I'm sorry," Char whispered as it sank home that this summons to Boston couldn't have come at a worse time.

"Are you? It seems to me you're rather eager to hightail it out of here."

"That's not true. I hate it. But I can't refuse to go. Especially not when I'm planning to ask for a promotion in the near future."

"If *my* office had called today, I would have refused to give up spending this time with you."

"Keith, be reasonable!" she pleaded, laughing nervously. "*You* can refuse because you're the boss. I'm not."

He scowled. "You didn't even *ask* if they'd be willing to wait an extra day."

"At Brannon-Hale, you don't ask that kind of thing."

"Sounds like a delightful place to work," he said sneeringly.

"That's hardly the point."

"Maybe it is."

"Listen," she said desperately. "Whatever you mean by that, I don't have time to talk about it right now! I've got to catch a plane to Boston. But I don't want to walk out of here with us both hurting and mad at each other." Her eyes pleaded with him.

There was a tense moment of silence, and then Keith sighed. "Hell, I don't want that either."

"Then please accept the fact that no matter how much I want to stay, I have to go. But I can try to get back this evening in time for a late dinner . . . if you still want me here."

"Tonight? Of course I want you here, you crazy woman." He charged across the room and hauled her into his arms. It felt so good to be back where she belonged, hugged hard against his solid chest. "I was afraid I might not see you again for *days*," he confessed.

"Nobody can keep me away from you for that long." She reached up and drew his head down to hers, kissing him with all the love and need she was feeling inside. "And that reminds me," she said a breathless moment later. "Though I would have preferred *not* to go to Boston today, at least this will give me the earliest possible chance to ask for a better assignment schedule. And I intend to get it, too!"

"Somehow that's not much consolation right now," Keith said wryly. "Damn, but I hate to see you go, even for one day." He rested his cheek against hers and whispered, "Hurry home, goddess."

"I will, love. Believe me, I will."

Char stared in horrified disbelief at the bald, bespectacled man behind the eight-foot mahogany desk. "Let me get this straight, sir. You called me here to reprimand me because of unsubstantiated rumors about my personal life?"

"Hardly unsubstantiated, Ms. Smith. After your romantic involvement with Mr. Keith Webb was first mentioned to us by his receptionist, who seemed to expect us to be *pleased* by the news, we made discreet inquiries among the other employees at the Webb Company. Apparently your relationship was no secret."

"It was no secret because we had nothing to hide!" She was shaking so hard with rage and humiliation that she could scarcely stand. "So long as Mr. Webb was my client, our relationship was a purely professional one, despite our admittedly warm feelings for one another."

Mr. Brannon frowned. "I would hardly describe as 'purely professional' a relationship that began several months *before* your assignment at Mr.

Webb's company, and that led to the breakup of Mr. Webb's engagement to another girl."

"That's not true! He was never engaged, and we never even met until—" She broke off as a sense of hopelessness invaded her. The incredible tangle of lies she'd agreed to for Keith's and Debbie's sakes suddenly seemed to be tightening like a noose around her neck. Mr. Brannon would never believe she hadn't met Keith until a few weeks ago, because everybody in Webb Falls would swear that they'd met long before that. How could she possibly explain?

"Ms. Smith, do you *deny* that you and Mr. Keith Webb were lovers?"

She bit her lip. *Oh, dear.* "No, but—"

"Then there's nothing more to be said. We at Brannon-Hale do not tolerate that kind of fraternization between our consultants and clients. Out of consideration for your previous excellent record with our firm, we will not request your resignation. However, such a flagrant dereliction of our professional code of conduct cannot go unpenalized. Effective immediately, you will be placed on probationary status, with a significant reduction in pay."

"Reduction in pay? But I haven't done anything wrong!" she cried. "Keith and I were never lovers while he was my client."

"The sordid details of your affair hardly matter, Ms. Smith. We are—"

"How dare you?" Char demanded. "There's nothing sordid about my love for Keith! And what do you mean, the *details* don't matter? How can the truth not matter?"

He gave her a pained, impatient look. "What concerns us is that your indiscreet, unprofessional conduct has created an appearance of impropriety that could compromise the reputation of Brannon-Hale."

"I see," she said bitterly. "So you don't really give a damn whether or not I actually slept with a client. All that bothers you is the fact that people think I did."

"Now, Ms. Smith," he said, hedging.

"Well, I think your attitude stinks! And you can take your probationary status and your pay cut and—" She stopped herself. A resignation should be cool, dignified, and professional, she decided. "I have no desire to continue working for a firm that cares more about appearances than it does about ethics. My resignation will be on your desk in half an hour." She turned and walked to the door.

"You're making a mistake, Ms. Smith." Mr. Brannon rose to his feet. "And you're going to regret it."

"No. The mistake was yours. And if I wanted to, I could sue the pants off you." She leveled a contemptuous glance at the portion of his pin-striped trousers that showed above the massive mahogany desk. "Only, in your case, it wouldn't be worth it."

So much for the dignified, professional approach, she thought as she walked out the door.

What have I done? Char asked herself as the plane braked to a stop on the runway in Albany. The adrenaline rush brought on by rage and indignation had long since faded. So, too, had her sense of exhilaration at standing up to Mr. Brannon's unjust accusations and hypocritical disciplinary measures. Now she was just plain scared at what she'd gotten herself into. Or *out* of, in this case.

Panic washed over her in black, choking waves as she drove out of the airport parking lot and headed for Webb Falls. She was out of a job. Unemployed. There would be no more paychecks. No more health benefits. No more pension. All her illusions of financial security were tumbling around her like a house of cards. She felt like a helpless child again.

And it was all Keith's fault. If only she hadn't listened to him, she thought, none of this would have happened. He'd promised to keep her involvement in the scheme to help Debbie at a minimum. He'd insisted that she would be able to keep a low profile. And then he'd turned around and announced to practically the whole world that he was in love with her! He'd kissed her in public. No wonder the talk had gotten back to Brannon-Hale. All along, Keith had shown a reckless disregard for her career and her reputation. And now she'd lost her job because of him.

"Now, Char, be *fair*," a faint inner voice chided. "You can't blame Keith for everything. After all, you chose to take part in the charade, even though you knew it was unwise and unprofessional. And as for those kisses, neither the public ones nor the private ones were exactly one-sided. Besides, it was *Keith* who'd respected your professional ethics enough to insist on postponing the lovemaking until he was no longer your client. He had done that when you hadn't the strength."

But suddenly Char was in no mood for fairness. "Whatever I did, it was because of his no-good sexy smile and his darn sweet-talk." She burst into tears. "I was a fool."

So why was she heading as fast as she could back to the little town and the white frame farmhouse where the man with the no-good sexy smile was waiting for her? Char couldn't say. Until now, whenever she'd been in dire need of comfort, reassurance, and love, she'd turned to her family. Now she was instinctively counting on Keith to give her those things. Maybe it didn't make sense when she also happened to be furious with him, but logic was another thing she wasn't in the mood for.

Keith met her at the door. "You look like you've been through a war," he said as he pulled her into his arms. "What happened, love? What did those bas—"

"Shh." She put her trembling fingers against his lips. "I don't even want to talk about it. Not yet. Just hold me, Keith." She pressed her face against his shoulder, breathing in the scent of him, feeling his warmth and strength enfold her. She found herself wishing they never had to talk about it at all, wishing it didn't matter. But she knew it did.

He held her tightly, running his hand soothingly up and down her spine. When he gently tipped her head back, his eyes darkened with concern as he studied her white face and shell-shocked blue eyes. "You'd better sit down before you keel over," he said gruffly.

He drew her unresisting body into the living room and lowered her onto the soft, slate-blue cushions of the sofa. "I'll get you a drink," he announced, heading through the French doors into the dining room.

"Better make it a stiff one," she said, closing her eyes. Mere seconds later he was back, shoving an ice-cold glass into her hands. She tried to smile. "That was quick. But . . . pineapple chunks and a little paper umbrella on top?" she asked incredulously.

"It's a piña colada."

"I know. I just can't believe you whipped up this fancy tropical concoction in two seconds flat. It's hardly what I was expecting when I asked for a 'stiff drink.' Not that I don't like it," she added hastily, taking a nervous gulp of the rum, pineapple, and coconut mixture.

A rosy flush had crept over his cheeks. "Actually, I had it mixed ahead of time. You see . . ." He made a vague, embarrassed gesture toward the dining room, and Char's gaze finally lifted and then focused on what lay beyond the French doors.

"Oh, dear heaven," she said.

The dining room had been transformed into a veritable jungle of potted palm trees and hanging vines. The table was set with an eclectic touch; fine china and crystal on woven-grass place mats, with a showy centerpiece of exotic orchids. A fake stuffed parrot was perched on a stand near the doorway, and a large print of a flamboyant Gauguin painting was displayed on the wall next to a beach-at-sunset travel poster.

"Tahiti?" she croaked.

Keith ducked his head. "It seemed like a good idea at the time," he said sheepishly. "I didn't realize you'd come back tonight practically in tears, or I'd have planned something more low-key."

"I think it's sweet. And romantic." In fact, it was everything that Keith himself was, she thought. Whimsical, touching, and irresistible. And, like the drink in her hand, potent and intoxicating. No wonder she'd fallen in love with him. No wonder she'd let him bewitch her into making the mistakes that had cost her her job. Tears welled up in her eyes and spilled down her cheeks.

"Damn. Now you *are* crying. Char, what's wrong? You've got to tell me!" He sat beside her on the sofa and cradled her in his arms.

"It's my job," she confessed, sobbing. "I quit Brannon-Hale."

Keith was silent for so long that she tipped her head to peer at him through tear-soaked lashes. He seemed to be struggling to find the proper expression to wear on his face.

"Well, aren't you going to say anything?" she asked in a choked voice.

"I know how much that job meant to you, Char. But . . ."

"But?"

"I think you made the right decision."

"Decision?" Her voice rose ominously.

"If they wouldn't let you cut down on your travel assignments, then quitting was the only real answer. Don't you see? It makes everything so much easier." He smiled encouragingly.

"Easier?" Easier for whom? she thought in outrage. Not for her, certainly! She felt like strangling him. He was supposed to be offering her sympathy and comfort, not jumping for joy.

"Now we'll have more time together, goddess! In fact, we can . . ." He leaped up off the couch and hurried into the dining room. When he came back, he held a gift-wrapped package. "I'd planned to give you this later, but now seems like the right time."

He had to be kidding. The *right* time? Char felt numb with hurt and anger as he placed the gift in her lap. How could he be so blind to her feelings? Did he expect her to *celebrate* losing her job?

"Go on, open it," he coaxed.

Mindlessly, mechanically, she stripped away the bright ribbons and shiny paper and opened the box. Inside lay two airline ticket folders. She stared down at them without saying a word.

"Look, Char." Eagerly he showed her the typewritten itinerary on the ticket jacket. "Tahiti. Nothing's stopping us now. We can be together on a tropical island paradise, alone on our own private stretch of beach."

She kept her head bowed so he couldn't see the

wounded anger in her eyes. "I'm afraid Tahiti is out of the question," she said in a low, shaking voice. "I can't afford a trip right now. Thanks to you, I'm unemployed. I'll need every penny I've got just to live on while I start looking for a new job."

"But, Char!" He laughed. "Of course I'm not asking you to help pay for the trip! It's a gift. And there's no need to start job-hunting right away—this is the perfect opportunity to take an extralong vacation! In fact—"

"I can't possibly accept that kind of gift," she cut in sharply. "And being unemployed is nothing like a vacation! Though I don't suppose the head of the Webb Company has ever been in a position to understand the difference," she added bitterly.

He looked confused. "If you're worried about your financial situation, don't be. What's mine is yours." He must have sensed how she stiffened at that, because he tried to forestall her refusal. "Dammit, Char, don't say you can't accept it! What's wrong with a man wanting to share everything he has with the woman he loves? And as for the trip to Tahiti, what's wrong with a husband giving his bride a honeymoon to remember?"

"*What?*" Her head jerked back, and she looked up to find him regarding her with tender exasperation.

"I'm trying to ask you to marry me, Char. I love you and I want to spend a lifetime making magic with you, hearing your laughter, and carrying you off into the sunset. Please, goddess, say yes?"

Pain stabbed through her at his words. Part of her wanted to say yes, wanted it so much she could feel the word forming like a kiss on her lips. But the word that came out was different: "No."

Keith's jaw dropped, and he blinked. "No?"

"No." She was trembling.

He turned pale. "I thought you loved me."

"I did—I *do*! But life isn't all sex and sunsets and laughter, Keith. It's not all magic. Sometimes things go wrong. Terribly wrong. And when they do, you need someone you can count on to help you through the bad times. Someone who understands you and cares about your feelings. I thought you were that person for me, but now I see I was wrong."

"What do you mean, *wrong*?"

"I can't count on you for the bad times," she said simply. "And without that, a marriage isn't worth much."

"Dammit, Char, what gives you the right to say you can't count on me? I'm not like your father! I'd never let you down the way he did."

"No, you're not like my father," she said sadly. "But you've already let me down. Do you have any idea how devastated I feel about losing my job? No, because you don't care. You haven't even tried to understand my feelings. All you can think about is how convenient it'll be for *you*!" Her voice broke.

"*What*? That's ridiculous! All I've done is support your decision to quit working for a company that's been taking advantage of you! I thought I was cheering you up by talking about our future. I *assumed* you'd be as pleased as I was that we could spend more time together." He turned away from her to stare out the window at the darkness. "It seems I was wrong."

Char stood up, fists clenched at her sides. "You keep talking about this big 'decision' of mine. Well, it wasn't. Frankly, I didn't have much choice. Not after they called me on the carpet over my indiscreet and unprofessional affair with my latest client!"

"*What*?" He whirled to face her.

"Oh, yes. Your employees were quite happy to supply them with the 'facts.' It seems you and I have been carrying on a torrid romance for over four months now, and you even broke your engagement to another woman because of me."

"But that's not true," he said hoarsely.

"Exactly what *I* said. Unfortunately, after almost three weeks of pretending that it *was* true, denying it was rather awkward. Besides, the truth didn't matter to Brannon-Hale—all they cared about was what people believed had happened."

"My God! I had no idea—"

"*Obviously.*" Her voice was bitter. "You never took my fears for my reputation and career very seriously, did you? You never tried very hard to keep our relationship quiet, because it wasn't your own life you were playing games with!"

"Char, I . . . I'm sorry. I feel terrible. But . . . it's hardly the end of the world, is it?"

She felt as if he'd hit her right between the eyes. "Not for you, apparently," she said, trying to hold back the tears. "But it's definitely the end for *us.* You can't possibly love me, because you don't even *know* me. My job meant the world to me! And if you—"

"Dammit, Char, I think you're overreacting here! Your job at Brannon-Hale wasn't worth crying over, much less losing each other over!"

That did it. She walked to the door.

"Thanks," she said. "You've just made it crystal clear that you have no respect for me, my work, or my feelings. There's nothing more to say. Except good-bye."

She slammed the door behind her and ran to her car. The tires kicked up gravel as she gunned the engine and drove away.

Eleven

Char stormed in the front door of the Benson place, causing Steve, Ann, and Lisa, who were eating pizza in front of the TV set, to look up in surprise.

"Gosh, aren't you supposed to be with *him*?" Ann asked.

Char ignored that. "Where's Faye? I need to settle my bill for the room."

"She's out with Mr. Foster. Gosh, are you moving in with Mr. Webb?"

The ache in her chest intensified. "No, I'm leaving town." Her voice threatened to give way on the last word, and she quickly turned her back on their astonished faces and headed for the stairs.

"Did you two have a fight?" Ann called after her.

"Yes." She ran up the stairs as if her life depended on it. It was time to start packing. She dragged her suitcases out of the closet and opened them on the bed. She was briskly removing a pile of clothing from the mahogany chest of drawers when she caught the scent of dried rose petals.

Petals from the six dozen roses Keith had given

her. She'd been saving them in a flowered china bowl on top of the dresser, and their scent was sharp and sweet and cruel. "Remember the moon-light, the roses, and me," he'd written. Oh, yes, she remembered. How could she have let something so magical slip away? She bowed her head over the bowl of petals and sobbed like a child.

What have I done? she asked herself for the second time that day. Only, this time, she knew she'd walked out on a whole lot more than she had at Brannon-Hale. She could eventually replace her old job with a new one. But nobody could replace Keith. Not ever.

"Char?" At the sound of Lisa's voice just outside the door, she froze in horror. Though a few weeks of living under the same roof had led to an unspoken truce and a sort of grudging respect between Char and the resourceful twelve-year-old, there was no one she was *less* willing to face at that moment. She was at the end of her emotional rope, and dealing with Lisa Benson would take more strength than she had left.

"Char?" Lisa knocked once more, and then opened the door and peeped inside. "Have you seen a—oh! You're crying!" she said, sounding fright-ened. Next thing Char knew, a small, freckled hand was tugging at her elbow. "What's wrong? Want me to try and call Mom and tell her to come home?"

"No, of course not, Lisa. I'll be fine in just a minute," she lied.

"But she's so good to talk to when you feel *real* bad," Lisa urged. The intensely worried expression on her thin, freckled face made Char remember how scary it was for a child to see an adult cry.

"I'm sure she is." Char reached for a Kleenex and wiped her eyes. "My mom's like that too." She felt a sudden longing for her mother's outspoken, unpredictable advice. What would her mother suggest she do about Keith? she wondered.

"Oh? Where does she live?" asked Lisa.

"Milwaukee." If Lisa wanted to make small talk, that was fine with Char. As long as she didn't ask any tough questions.

"That's pretty far away," Lisa said.

"Yes, but we talk on the phone a lot."

"Oh." There was a moment of silence, and Char saw that Lisa's eyebrows were furrowed in thought. "What's your dad's name?" the girl asked finally.

"You mean my stepfather? David Haugen."

"Oh. Not Smith, huh? Well, I've got to go take care of something. Don't cry anymore, Char." Lisa hurried to the door, and then hesitated. "What's it like?" she asked shyly. "Having a stepfather, I mean?"

"It all depends. For us, it was great. We wanted a new father very much, and Dad was everything we could have asked for. He made us and our mother very happy."

"We might have a stepfather soon," Lisa confided. "If Mom and Mr. Foster get married. He's nice, don't you think?"

"They don't come much nicer than Bill," Char agreed.

Lisa nodded. "Well, so long. Oh, I almost forgot—if you see a white rat in here, don't scream, or anything, because Eek freaks if you scream."

"Eek . . . freaks?"

"Yeah. He goes bananas and runs all over the place. Like this morning when Mom did the vacuuming. I think he might've ducked in here and got shut in."

"I see. Well, I promise I'll be on the alert for him. And I'll try not to scream."

Several minutes later Char was still casting nervous glances around the room, when Lisa hollered up the stairs, "Cha-ar! Pho-one!"

"Who is it?" she called. *Please let it be Keith*, she was praying as she dashed down the stairs.

"It's your mom," Lisa announced, handing her the phone.

Char clutched the receiver as if it were a lifeline. Though the caller wasn't Keith, at least now she had her mother's shoulder to cry on. Sort of. "Mom? You must be psychic!" she exclaimed.

"Poppycock! A person doesn't have to be *psychic* to pick up the phone when it rings."

"When it rings? But—"

"Somebody named Lisa just called and said you needed to talk to me and that she'd put you on."

"Oh, yeah, she 'put me on,' all right." *The darn lovable little monkey*, Char thought.

"So what's all this Lisa's been telling me about you having a fight with your boyfriend? Last time I heard from you, you didn't even *have* a boyfriend."

"No, and now I don't have one *again*," she said forlornly. "Oh, Mom, I'm so miserable and I don't know what to do!"

"You'd better tell me the whole story, dear."

It wasn't an easy story to tell. Char hadn't realized how complicated it all was until she tried explaining it to her mom. And she found she had to skip certain details here and there, because there were some things you just didn't tell your mother. Let Mom figure those parts out for herself.

"So then I told him there was nothing more to say except good-bye, and I walked out the door and drove away," she concluded. "But now all I can think of is how much I love him and how wonderful he is and how happy we were together," she said tearfully. "So tell me, Mom, should I forgive him?"

"*Forgive him?* Don't talk hogwash, Char! You've behaved like an ass and now you'd better skedaddle back out to his place and ask him to forgive *you*!"

"But, Mom, haven't you been listening? It was because of him that I lost my job!"

"Good riddance! And the real reason you lost that job was because you followed your heart and tried to help somebody!" her mother exclaimed indignantly. "You chose human needs and emotions over the good of the company, and there's no room for that kind of choice at *that place* where you used to work. Just look at the way they ran you ragged for five whole years with never a thought for your personal life!"

"Now you sound just like Keith." But Char couldn't deny that her mother was making a lot of sense.

"Great minds sometimes think alike, dear."

"But if Keith really cared about me, he would have been more careful to keep our relationship a secret! And then Brannon-Hale wouldn't have found out."

"It's hard to keep love a secret. Besides, I thought the whole point of all the make-believe was to convince everybody in Webb Falls that you two were crazy about each other. So how *could* you keep it a secret?"

Char swallowed. "I never thought of it that way."

"I doubt if Keith did either." Her mother sighed. "People in love aren't always terribly rational."

"Don't rub it in." The full impact of what she'd done finally hit her. "Oh, Mom, I was so angry with Keith for not understanding my feelings, but I wasn't really listening to what he was saying either! Otherwise, how could I have walked out on him just because he told me the truth? He was right—my job wasn't even worth crying over! There are lots of consulting firms I could work for, or I could even start my own. But there's only one man I'll ever be happy with, and that's Keith."

"Then don't you think it's about time you told him so?"

She took a deep breath. "Yes."

After a hasty "Thank you and I love you, Mom," she hung up and dashed upstairs to get her car keys. Just as she reached her door, she heard a bloodcurdling scream. A split second later, a large white rat darted out of Ann Benson's room and zigzagged frantically up and down the hallway. Eek had freaked.

Almost instantly Lisa was on the scene, scooping her panicked pet into her arms and murmuring soothing words of comfort. "Poor baby," she crooned. "Don't you know better than to hide in *her* room?"

"Lisa, you damn brat!" Ann shrieked from her doorway. "I'm gonna kill that rat of yours. Just look what he made me do!" Bright fuchsia nail polish was splashed all down the front of her white beaded sweater.

"You touch one whisker on Eek's face and I'll tell Fred what you said about his car!" Lisa threatened.

Ann bared her teeth, snarled, and slammed the door.

"Serves her right," muttered Lisa. "Practically the minute you got home, she called up Debbie to tell her about your fight with Mr. Webb."

Char groaned. "Well, I'm about to go back and try to make up with him, so I hope that phone call won't be much help to Debbie. But *your* call to my mother was a big help to me. Thanks, Lisa."

"No prob," said Lisa.

Two minutes later, Char raced out of the house and hopped into her car. Her hand shook with impatience as she turned the key in the ignition. Her mind was full of the words she'd say to Keith as soon as she reached him. And then she discovered that her car wouldn't start.

She couldn't believe it. All her future happiness depended on getting out to Keith's place right away, so how could this be happening? Her car *had* to start! But it didn't. And then it occurred to her that this was no coincidence. Someone had been tampering with her car! And she thought she knew who.

After a quick check of the tailpipe, to make sure this wasn't a repeat of the easily solved fruit trick, she marched back to the house for a confrontation with her enemy. Somehow she wasn't surprised to see Steve Benson standing on the front porch with his arms folded across his chest, looking stubborn, embarrassed, and guilty as sin.

"What did you do to my car?" she demanded.

He squared his chin defiantly. "I fixed it so you won't be going anywhere for the next few days."

Her heart sank. "Dammit, Steve, I thought you had sense enough to realize you're only hurting yourself by acting this way! If Keith and I don't get back together, he might wind up with Debbie after all. Is that what you really want?"

"Of course not." Steve looked confused. "But that's the whole reason I put your car on the blink. So you couldn't leave town right away, like you were planning. I figured you might change your mind if you stuck around long enough."

"I don't believe this! I've *already* changed my mind, Steve! And I need my car so I can go see Keith and make up our quarrel. So will you please fix it?"

"Oh, shoot." He shook his head. "I can't. It's going to need a whole lot of work, I'm afraid."

"Then what am I going to do?" she asked with a wail. "I've *got* to see Keith tonight!"

Steve hesitated. "Well, there's the old Chevy out

in the shed that I've been tinkering with all summer," he said doubtfully. "I've got it to the point where it might make it out to Webb's place."

"I'll take it."

"I'm afraid you'd better let me do the driving. That car's got to be handled just right, and even then she's pretty unpredictable."

Char sighed. "If you say so. But once we get there, just drop me off and head back home, okay?" She figured that way Keith would be stuck with her, so he'd *have* to listen to her apologies.

"Okay," Steve said.

But that wasn't how it turned out. The old car broke down three times on the way to Keith's, and twice Steve was able to get it going again . . . just barely. By then it was a wonder Char's knuckles weren't worn to the bone, due to her perpetual gnawing on them. When the car conked out for the third time, it was on the steep driveway up to the farmhouse, and that was that. It wasn't budging an inch farther.

Char was so nervous and impatient to see Keith that she felt like a basket case, but she helped Steve push the car off to the side of the driveway before heading for the house. "You'd better come on up and use the phone," she told him. She had no idea what Keith would think when he saw Steve with her, but what else could she do? Leave him in the car all night? Ask him to walk home?

As they set off up the hill, Char felt the tension knotting inside her. So far, this had been the most emotionally draining day of her life. And what happened in the next few minutes would determine whether she wound up the happiest woman on earth or the most miserable one. *Oh, dear,* she thought, smoothing the rumpled, mud-stained skirt of the suit she'd worn to Boston and back again. *This is it.*

Char didn't recognize the cream-colored BMW parked on the gravel drive in front of the farmhouse. Steve frowned. "That's Debbie's car," he said.

Oh, dear, Char thought again. *Another complication.* Her heart went out to Keith as she realized what he must be going through. The odds were good that right this minute Debbie was trying to renew the relationship he'd tried so hard to end painlessly.

She and Steve were both very quiet as they approached the house. The front door was open, and the screen door didn't block the sound of voices from inside.

"What do I have to say to get it through your head that I'm not interested?" Keith's harsh voice exploded over the soft chirping of the crickets on the lawn. Char and Steve halted on the flagstone walkway. She didn't have the courage to interrupt the conversation inside. And she knew she shouldn't be eavesdropping. But . . .

"I know you're bitter right now because of *her*," Debbie's voice said soothingly. "But you mustn't judge us all by one woman. She was an outsider, Keith. She didn't understand you or Webb Falls. And she was selfish. All she cared about was her career."

Char wanted to sink through the flagstones. Was that really how she came across to people? she wondered, agonized. Was that how Keith saw her now?

"How dare you?" Keith's words were bitten off with barely controlled fury. "Don't try to tell *me* about the woman I love! She's got more warmth and passion and generosity than you could ever imagine. Sure, she cares about her job, but she was willing to put it on the line to help someone she'd never even met. Someone who damn sure wasn't worth the trouble!"

Char reached for the porch railing and held on to it for dear life. *Oh, Keith*, she thought, choked with love for him. His defense of her made her want to cry, especially since she knew it wasn't completely deserved.

"I don't know what you're talking about," said Debbie.

"Obviously. But it's time you learned. I've sacrificed enough happiness—both my own and Char's—trying to shield a spoiled child from reality! The truth is, Debbie, I've never had any romantic interest in you. *Never*," he repeated. "And it has nothing to do with some limp that nobody cares about but you!"

There were several seconds of overwhelming silence from inside the house, and Char heard a rustle of movement beside her as Steve stepped toward the porch and then stopped, his fists clenched at his sides.

"But why did you ask me out in the first place?" Debbie finally asked in a voice thick with tears.

"That was Aunt Agnes's idea. I thought of it as just a friendly gesture. When I saw that you were reading way too much into it, I tried to let you down easily by telling you I was in love with another woman."

"Charlotte Smith." Debbie's voice was bitter.

"Right. But, as you guessed at the time, I was lying. Char and I had never met."

Debbie gasped. "But—"

"I got the shock of my life when Char showed up in Webb Falls. To make a long story short, she generously agreed to go along with the charade and pretend we were in love. It didn't take long for pretense to become reality."

"But why bother to pretend? Just so you could trick me and laugh at me behind my back?"

"Of course not, dammit! We did it so your feelings wouldn't be hurt by learning the truth."

"You m-mean you *felt s-sorry for me?*" Debbie wailed in outrage and humiliation.

Keith hesitated. "Well, yes, but—"

Steve shoved past Char and charged up the porch steps like an angry bull, sending the screen door banging as he ran inside. A split second later, Char gathered her wits and ran after him. She saw Keith and Debbie standing in the doorway to the dining room, and Steve moving toward them. She caught a glimpse of Keith's startled face and then the leap of gladness in his eyes as he saw *her*.

And then Steve hit him.

"How dare you feel sorry for her? Can't you see she doesn't need your pity?" Steve shouted at Keith, who lay on the floor rubbing his jaw and looking utterly astonished.

"What the hell is going on?" Keith muttered under his breath to Char when she knelt down beside him amid the wreckage of a potted palm and the fuzzy fake parrot he'd knocked over as he fell.

"Oh, Keith, are you all right?" she whispered anxiously.

"I've been better." His eyes questioned her as he reached for her hand.

"Can't you see how beautiful she is?" Steve continued furiously, gesturing toward where Debbie stood in stricken silence. "Any man in his right mind—unghh!" He groaned suddenly, clutching his hand and sinking to his knees. "My hand," he said with a moan. "I think I broke it on Webb's face!"

"Serves him right," Keith muttered, gingerly running his palm along his jaw where it was starting to swell.

"You need some ice to put on that," Char said, shifting her weight so she could stand up. "And I'll get some for Steve's hand too," she added as an afterthought. But Keith's arm went around her so tightly, she couldn't move.

"I don't need any damn ice, Char. Just you."

Her heart somersaulted at the rough, husky timbre of his voice and the hungry look in his green eyes. His arm cradled her in a ring of fire, and she felt her bones go soft. Even if she'd wanted to, she couldn't have stood up after that.

"Stay with me, goddess?"

"Oh, yes," she whispered. "I'll stay."

Keith's kiss engulfed her in a sweet, heady tide of magical sensation. All the love in the world seemed to flow from his lips to hers and back again, forging a link that no future quarrel could ever break.

It wasn't until they drew apart a few minutes later that Char remembered Steve and Debbie. "Oh, dear!" she mumbled, blushing guiltily. She darted a hasty, embarrassed glance over to where Steve had collapsed in pain, and was surprised and relieved to see Debbie applying ice cubes wrapped in a kitchen towel to his injured hand. Neither Debbie nor Steve was paying any attention to the other couple in the room.

The girl's face as she bent over Steve held an anxious tenderness. "Oh, Steve, you shouldn't have done it," she softly scolded. "A guy who's going to be a doctor has to take care of his hands."

"I couldn't let him get away with saying those things to you," Steve said, gazing up at her with such open adoration that Debbie's cheeks turned pink.

"Steve, I never realized . . ." Her sentence trailed off in confusion, but the warmth in her eyes made it clear that Debbie had no objection to discovering that Steve was in love with her. "You were wonderful," she said shyly, resting her hand on his good arm, and Steve looked as though he'd just died and gone to heaven.

Char felt a lump in her throat as she turned back to Keith. "Isn't it sweet?" she whispered.

"*Sweet*? Are you referring to the kid who almost dislocated my jaw, and the girl who's been a pain in my neck for the past six months?" he demanded in an incredulous whisper.

"Yep." She shrugged apologetically. "You can call me a sentimental, romantic fool, but—"

"Char, you're a sentimental, romantic fool. And I love you." His arm tightened around her shoulders. "Can you forgive me for letting you down?"

"There's nothing to forgive. You didn't let me down—I was just too scared and angry to understand what you were saying."

"But you're not scared and angry anymore?"

She smiled and shook her head.

"Good. Because I'm about to propose to you again, and I'd hate for you to misunderstand. Have you reconsidered, Char? Will you marry me?"

"Oh, Keith, yes!" she said, watching as the faint lines of uncertainty were smoothed away around his mouth and eyes. "But you've got to let me tell you how sorry I am that I acted like such a dunderhead."

"No."

"No?"

"I won't let you tell me how sorry you are. First things first." And he kissed her with such hungry passion that Char forgot everything but the delight of kissing him back. This time, after countless minutes spent blissfully lost in his arms, she was recalled to an awareness of her surroundings by an impatient cough behind her.

"I'm taking Steve to a doctor," Debbie announced

stiffly. "In case you two hadn't noticed, his hand could use some medical attention."

"Um, right," Char said breathlessly. "That's a good idea."

"You'd better send me the bill," Keith ordered gruffly.

"But, sir—" Steve protested.

"Don't argue. I find that getting engaged to Char is well worth a sore jaw and a doctor's bill."

"I see," Steve said. "Congratulations." Char saw him give Debbie's hand a reassuring squeeze, and Debbie squeezed back.

"Thanks," said Keith. After the younger couple had left together, he turned to Char. "Now, goddess, where were we?"

"We had just gotten ourselves engaged."

"Oh, yes." He grinned from ear to ear, and pulled her close against him. "I remember now. I was about to carry you off into the sunset."

He stood up, bringing Char to her feet beside him. She had no intention of pointing out that the sun had set several hours ago. He leaned over the dining-room table and picked an orchid from the centerpiece of tropical flowers. Tucking it behind her ear, he asked huskily, "Now, goddess, how about that honeymoon in Tahiti?"

"I can't wait."

"Neither can I." He lifted her in his arms and headed for the stairs.

THE EDITOR'S CORNER

Do you grumble as much as I do about there being too few hours in the day? Time. There just never seems to be enough of it! That seemed especially to be the case a few weeks ago when we were sitting here facing a scheduling board with every slot filled for months and months . . . and an embarrassment of goodies (finished LOVESWEPT manuscripts, of course). But, then, suddenly, it occurred to us that the real world limitations of days and months didn't necessarily apply to a publishing schedule. Voilà! 1986 got rearranged a bit as we created a thirteenth month in the year for a unique LOVESWEPT publishing event. Our thirteenth month features three special romances going on sale October 15, 1986.

What's so remarkable that it warrants the creation of a month? Another "first" in series romance from LOVESWEPT: A trio of love stories by three of your favorite LOVESWEPT authors—Fayrene Preston, Kay Hooper, and Iris Johansen. **THE SHAMROCK TRINITY!** Fayrene, Kay, and Iris together "founded" the Delaney dynasty—its historical roots, principal members, settings, and present day heirs. (Those heirs are three of the most exciting men you'd ever want to meet in the pages of romances—Burke, York, and Rafe.) Armed with genealogies, sketches of settings, research notes they'd made on a joint trip to Arizona in which the books were to be set, each author then went off alone to create her own book in her own special style. There are common secondary characters, running gags through the three books. They can be read in any order, stand alone if the other two books are not read. Each book features appearances by the heroes of the other two books, each is set during the same span of time—and yet, no one gives away the end of the other books. This is a fascinating trinity of stories, indeed, very clever and well-crafted, and packing all the wallop you expect in a love story by Fayrene or Kay or Iris.

Don't miss these extraordinary love stories. Ask your bookseller to be sure to save the three books of **THE SHAMROCK TRINITY** for you. They are:

RAFE, THE MAVERICK
LOVESWEPT #167
By Kay Hooper

(continued)

YORK, THE RENEGADE
LOVESWEPT #168
By Iris Johansen

BURKE, THE KINGPIN
LOVESWEPT #169
By Fayrene Preston

Now, as I said above, there is an embarrassment of goodies around here. And four excellent examples are your LOVESWEPT romances for next month.

Leading off is witty Billie Green with **GLORY BOUND**, LOVESWEPT #155. Gloria Wainwright had a secret ... and Alan Spencer, a blind date arranged by her matchmaking father, was a certain threat to keeping that secret. He was just too darned attractive, too irresistible, and the only way to maintain her "other life" was for Glory to avoid him—in fact, to disappear from Alan's world. But he tracked down the elusive lady whose various disguises hadn't repelled him as Glory intended, but only further intrigued him. When Alan and Glory come face to face in her bedroom—under the wildest circumstances imaginable—firecrackers truly do go off between these two. This romance is another sheer delight from Billie Green.

After a long absence from our list, the versatile Marie Michael is back with **NO WAY TO TREAT A LOVER**, LOVESWEPT #156. This is the fastpaced, exciting—often poignant—love story of beautiful Charley (short for Charlotte) Tremayne and the deliciously compelling Reese McDaniel. After a madly passionate affair, Charley had disappeared to follow a dangerous life of intrigue. Now, she and Reese are thrown together again on the stage of a musical bound for Broadway. Charley tries to stay away from Reese—for his safety!—but cannot resist him! You'll want to give both of these endearing people a standing ovation as they overcome Charley's fears ... and a few other stumbling blocks fate throws in their way.

Peggy Webb's **DUPLICITY**, LOVESWEPT #157, is a delightfully humorous book that also will tug at your heartstrings. Dr. Ellen Stanford knows it is reckless to bring a perfect stranger home to pose as her fiance, but she just can't face another family reunion alone. Besides, the myste-

(continued)

rious Dirk is about as perfect as a man can get—as good looking as Tom Selleck, masterful yet tender, and one fabulous kisser! But Ellen is dedicated to her work, teaching sign language to a gorilla named Gigi, and Dirk is pledged to a way of life filled with dangerous secrets. How Dirk and Ellen work through their various deceptions will delight you and no doubt make you laugh out loud—especially when Gigi gets in the act as matchmaker!

Rounding out the month is another fabulous romance from Barbara Boswell! **ALWAYS AMBER,** LOVESWEPT #158, is a sequel to **SENSUOUS PERCEPTION,** LOVESWEPT #78. Remember Ashlee and Amber? They were the twins who were adopted in infancy by different families. In **SENSUOUS PERCEPTION,** Ashlee located her sister—and fell in love with Amber's brother. Now it's Amber's turn for romance. She has finally broken out of her shell and left the family banking business. The last person she expects to meet, much less be wildly attracted to, is Jared Stone, president of a bank that is her family's biggest rival. Amber doesn't quite trust Jared's intentions toward her, but can't deny her overwhelming need for him. You'll cheer Jared on as he passionately, relentlessly pursues Amber, until he finally breaks through her last inhibitions. . . . A breathless, delicious love story!

At long—wonderful—last the much awaited **SUNSHINE AND SHADOW** by Sharon and Tom Curtis will be published. This fabulous novel will be on sale during the first week of September. Be sure to look for it.

Have a glorious month of reading pleasure!

Warm regards,

Sincerely,

Carolyn Nichols

Carolyn Nichols
   Editor
LOVESWEPT
Bantam Books, Inc.
666 Fifth Avenue
New York, NY 10103

LOVESWEPT

Love Stories you'll never forget by authors you'll always remember

☐	21753	Stubborn Cinderalla #135 Eugenia Riley	$2.50
☐	21746	The Rana Look #136 Sandra Brown	$2.50
☐	21750	Tarnished Armor #137 Peggy Webb	$2.50
☐	21757	The Eagle Catcher #138 Joan Elliott Pickart	$2.50
☐	21755	Delilah's Weakness #139 Kathleen Creighton	$2.50
☐	21758	Fire In The Rain #140 Fayrene Preston	$2.50
☐	21759	Crescendo #141 A. Staff & S. Goldenbaum	$2.50
☐	21754	Trouble In Triplicate #142 Barbara Boswell	$2.50

Prices and availability subject to change without notice.

Buy them at your local bookstore or use this handy coupon for ordering:

Bantam Books, Inc., Dept. SW2, 414 East Golf Road, Des Plaines, Ill. 60016

Please send me the books I have checked above. I am enclosing $_____
(please add $1.50 to cover postage and handling). Send check or money order
—no cash or C.O.D.'s please.

Mr/Mrs/Miss _____

Address _____

City _____State/Zip _____

SW2—7/86

Please allow four to six weeks for delivery. This offer expires 1/87.

LOVESWEPT

Love Stories you'll never forget by authors you'll always remember

☐	21760	**Donovan's Angel #143** Peggy Webb	$2.50
☐	21761	**Wild Blue Yonder #144** Millie Grey	$2.50
☐	21762	**All Is Fair . . . #145** Linda Cajio	$2.50
☐	21763	**Journey's End #146** Joan Elliott Pickart	$2.50
☐	21751	**Once In Love With Amy #147** Nancy Holder	$2.50
☐	21749	**Always #148** Iris Johansen	$2.50
☐	21765	**Time After Time #149** Kay Hooper	$2.50
☐	21767	**Hot Tamales #150** Sara Orwig	$2.50

Prices and availability subject to change without notice.

Buy them at your local bookstore or use this handy coupon for ordering:

Bantam Books, Inc., Dept. SW3, 414 East Golf Road, Des Plaines, Ill. 60016

Please send me the books I have checked above. I am enclosing $_____ (please add $1.50 to cover postage and handling). Send check or money order —no cash or C.O.D.'s please.

Mr/Mrs/Miss_____

Address_____

City_____ State/Zip_____

SW3—7/86

Please allow four to six weeks for delivery. This offer expires 1/87.